RIDER OF THE DIM TRAILS

RIDER
OF THE
DIM TRAILS

By

Buck Billings

WILDSIDE PRESS

CONTENTS

RIDER OF THE DIM TRAILS

Chapter 1

FLIGHT

"How many, boys?"

Ran Hollis flipped the cards as they were called for, his bronzed face expressionless in the shadow of his wide hat. Hunch Watkins took two, Slim Hall three. Cal Taylor, their boss, owner of the big Cross-L, asked for one card and growled as he scanned it. Ran took two.

There was a tenseness in the air. Ran sensed it, just as he sensed Cal Taylor's hatred for himself. Watson and Hall eased their chairs back a trifle.

Less than a month previous, Ran had drifted into town. He bought a drink in Monk Holliday's big saloon and asked Monk about a job of riding. The saloon keeper was pessimistic.

"Things are jest about the same as farther west, where you come from," said Monk. "The hard winter and the drought's made ridin' jobs mighty scarce."

He glanced speculatively at Ran's slim, supple hands. "Tell you what, son," he went on, "I sorta like yore looks. I'll give you a job dealin' at my

9

poker table till somethin' turns up. You don't have to know any tricks—I run a straight game."

Ran took the job, and would have been fairly satisfied had it not been for Cal Taylor. Taylor owned the biggest ranch in the county and a bad reputation. He was ruthless, domineering, and had tough characters riding for him. It was whispered that the Cross-L was a clearing house for *marihuana* and Chinamen smuggled across the Line. There were also whispers of wide looping of which the Cross-L knew more than it cared to talk about. Taylor also owned much property in Mexico. The officials of the despotic Diaz government were friendly to him. All in all, Taylor was a hard citizen, not at all liked by his neighbors, who feared him because of his wealth, his influence and the questionable ways in which he used both.

Taylor gambled heavily and was a poor loser. For no reason at all he had developed an intense hatred for the young cowboy who dealt for Monk Holliday. Monk, however, advanced a reason of his own.

"That young feller is square and decent, and Taylor ain't, that's why," rumbled the burly saloon keeper, who feared no man.

The game went on. Taylor lost the pot to Ran, cursed viciously and called for a new deck. Slim Hall and Hunch Watkins exchanged stealthy glances.

Ran dealt a new hand, flipped the discards together and bet. Taylor glanced at him keenly.

"I'm callin'," he growled surlily.

Ran spread his hand on the table—"Aces up!"

With a wordless roar, Taylor slammed his cards down beside Ran's. *Three aces,* a trey and a six-spot. Ran stared at the *five aces* spread before his eyes. *"Taylor palmed an ace from the old deck and slipped it in!"* his mind clamored. Taylor's voice jerked him back in his chair:

"No wonder the house is winnin'! Five aces to a deck! You crooked tinhorn——"

Crash!

It wasn't Taylor's half-drawn Colt that thundered in the close room. Ran Hollis' right hand shot out. A stubby double-barreled derringer slid from his sleeve and spat flame almost before his fingers closed around it. Ran's wrist moved slightly and again the short gun boomed. He beat Slim Hall's draw, but Hunch Watkins' six went off so close that it blew Ran's hat from his head. The derringer was empty and Watkins was pressing trigger for another shot. He hesitated just the bare fraction of a second to steady his aim and that instant's delay was fatal: Hunch had forgotten that Ran Hollis was left-handed!

A smoking Colt in his left hand, the empty derringer still in his right, Ran moved backward from the table. He eyed the three silent forms on the floor as if wondering how they got there.

"*Freeze! All of you!*"

Ran started. The booming voice had sounded from behind him. He was aware that men had suddenly stiffened, some of them in grotesque positions.

"Hollis, come here—keep outa my line o' fire!"

Ran glanced over his shoulder. Behind him was the long bar and back of the bar and a little to one side stood Monk Holliday, owner of the saloon, his sawed-off ten-gauge shotgun taking in the whole room with the sweep of its yawning muzzles. Ran slipped the derringer in his vest pocket, picked up his hat and obliqued to the end of the bar. Holliday was hissing words, his voice little above a whisper, his lips moving not at all:

"Slip through the back room, you damn fool, get yore hoss and ride like hell! This outfit'll hang you shore once they break loose. There're Cross-L punchers here 'sides Watkins and Hall."

"But you. They'll——"

"Don't you worry 'bout me—nobody's goin' to make trouble for Monk Holliday—not in this county—but I won't be able to keep 'em offa you once they find out this scattergun's empty. Get goin', damn it!"

Ran got goin'. He knew Holliday was safe: the saloon keeper was a power in local politics and a hell-roarer with gun or knife. Nobody would try to make trouble for Monk.

But there were plenty who would make trouble for Hollis. Ran fully realized this as he saddled his tall black gelding in seconds of time. His bedroll was in place and his foot was in the stirrup when a crash of glass and a deep-toned roar sounded from the saloon. As he clattered past the stable, long lances of orange flame stabbed through the darkness and lead whistled all about him.

"June along, hoss," he told the black. "It's Mexico for ours. That Cross-L outfit jest about runs this here end of Arizona and I plugged their king-pin. Five aces! Guess I musta been asleep when Taylor called for a new deck. If it hadn't been for that sleeve-gun trick old Hassayampa Hawkins showed me when he taught me how to deal cyards, I'd be spreadin' my bedroll on the Big Range about now. Well, this is what comes of a cow chambermaid thinkin' he was the makin's of a big-time gambler. Guess you and me'll stick to business after this."

Huge and shadowy and blue in the starlight, the mountains of Mexico reared their mighty bulk against the southwestern sky. Their canyons and gorges and tangled thickets provided refuge for hunted men. Beyond were vast ranches where thousands of cattle roamed. The ranchers ruled them with feudal splendor. Plenty of work there for an efficient Arizona puncher.

"Guess I'll get me some velvet pants and a gold-tasseled *sombrero* and be a *vaquero* for a while," chuckled Ran as the pursuing hoofs of the Cross-L riders threaded away in thin whispers of sound. "After all a *vaquero* is jest a cowpoke in tight pants and a round-topped hat. June along, hoss, there's the Line t'other side them hills, and once acrost that we're safe."

That's what Ran *thought*. What he didn't realize was that Cross-L influence reached far into Mexico. Cal Taylor owned property there—much of it. He also stood high with the Diaz government; having done more than one favor for the unscrupulous old tyrant who was called *El Presidente* but who was in reality a czar of the middle ages flopped over into modern times. *El Presidente* and the Cross-L outfit had much in common, neither being troubled by a conscience and both firm in the belief that might made right. To which the down-trodden *peons* of Mexico could testify with scarred backs and scared whispers.

Ran kept to the mountains for a week, working south all the time. Hunger finally drove him into a little rat of a town festering in the shadow of an angry looking peak that appeared to resent its presence. Ran ate a meal in a frowsy dining room, looked into the door of an unsavory saloon, turned around—and looked into the muzzles of two six-shooters! He was caught settin' and didn't have a chance.

"Stickup?" he casually asked the dark face back of one of the guns.

"We are *serenos*," replied the other, "you will come with us."

Ran went with the policemen, minus his guns, to the office of the local *alcalde*. The mayor, a slim, aristocratic man with a cruel mouth and intolerant eyes, looked Ran over from head to foot.

"Lock him up," he ordered briefly before the cowboy could speak.

Ran stiffened, his blue eyes narrowed.

"Mind tellin' me what for?" he queried softly.

The *alcalde* glared.

"Speak when you are spoken to, and not before," he hissed in Spanish, which Ran understood very well.

"All right. I'm spoke to and I'm speakin'. What the hell——"

The *alcalde* gestured with a slim hand. One of the *serenos* standing behind Ran raised his gun and crashed the heavy barrel against the back of the puncher's head. Ran went out like a light.

The *alcalde* walked across the room and stared coldly at the crumpled form on the floor. He set the cruel Chihuahua spur decorating his right boot against the cowboy's cheek and ripped it down from cheekbone to chin. Blood poured from the jagged wound, spreading in an ever-widening pool over the rough boards. Ran shivered slightly and groaned. Then he slumped more loosely and lay still.

"*El carcel*," said the alcalde.

The two *serenos* lifted the limp and bloody figure and bore it off to the jail.

Chapter 2

EL CASCABEL

RAN came back to his senses with an aching head, empty pockets and a horribly sore face. It took him some little time to realize what had happened to him. The jailer's evil chuckle further enlightened him.

"The mark of *el alcalde*," leered the fellow, pointing a derisive finger at Ran's torn and swollen cheek. "It will last so long as life shall last, although that, *por Dios!* will not be for long."

The jailer seemed to take delight in telling the story and a few questions brought it all out.

A chill glitter birthed and grew in the cowboy's eyes as the tale unfolded, but his voice was soft and casual.

"Any idea why I'm here?"

The jailer chuckled wisely. "Assuredly! Shot you not the *Senor* Taylor of Arizona, the *amigo* of *El Presidente? El Presidente* forgets not his friends, nor those who injure them."

Ran nodded. "Uh-huh, I see. They gonna send me back to Arizona?"

17

The jailer's laugh rang loud.

"Ho! ho! And why? We have walls here in Sonora, and our brave *soldados* have rifles and pine to use them."

Ran understood perfectly. His back against a stone wall. A blindfold over his eyes. A squad of *El Presidente's* soldiers with loaded rifles. Then the word of command, the crash of the reports—and a crumpled, bloody bundle at the foot of the wall. The *"justice"* of *El Presidente!*

"When's it gonna happen?" he asked.

The other shrugged eloquent shoulders. "Who knows. Tomorrow, perhaps. Perhaps the day after tomorrow. But soon, *gringo*, soon! Content you, now. I go to prepare food. It behooves one not to take a long journey with hunger for his companion, eh?"

Sardonic laughter rang again as he bolted the heavy door. Ran felt a cold chill creep along his spine.

The jailer returned with bread as black and soggy as the underdone beans. Ran had little desire for food, but he forced himself to eat.

"Can't tell jest what'll happen," he mused, "and a feller does better on a full belly than when it's strainin' itself tryin' to get a grip on his backbone."

The jailer shoved his swarthy face against the iron grating.

"Waste not the bread," he cautioned. "Beans

I bring again when comes the night, but the bread is a full day's supply."

He bolted the outer door over the grating and left Ran alone with his thoughts, which were not pleasant.

An examination of the cell-like room convinced the cowboy that the jail was escape proof. The walls were of stone. The single window was small and heavily barred. The inner door was of iron bars. The outer a single sheet of steel. The jailer carried the keys jingling at his belt.

"If the horned toad'd unlock that inner door onct I'd take a chance on wallopin' him and walkin' out," Ran growled, "but he shoves stuff through the holes and keeps outa reach. If I jest had a gun!"

He peered longingly through a narrow crack between the outer door and the jam. Hanging on a nail back of the table that served the jailer for a desk he could see his belt and holstered sixes. There also was the little stubby derringer. The jailer had been much impressed with the short gun.

"I shall ask *El Alcalde* that I may keep it," he told Ran. "Such a weapon! Only by accident did we find it hidden in the sleeve. You must show me how works it from the sleeve and falls into the hand—after I have removed the loads."

"I'd show him how it *'works'* if I could get my chuck hooks on it!" Ran grated to himself.

He wandered to the window and stared at his black gelding tethered under a shed a few dozen yards distant. Saddle and bridle hung on a peg.

"Wonder who'll get them?" sighed the puncher. "Best hoss and best hull I ever owned."

He picked up the loaf of bread and eyed it distastefully.

"Black as the muzzle of a six-gun and damn near as hard!" he growled. "It——"

The words died on his lips. He stared at the dark loaf, a leaping light in his eyes.

"Mebbe I could!" he whispered. "Mebbe it would work!"

He glided to the door and listened. No sign of the jailer. He sat down with his back to the wall, where he could not be seen by anyone peering through the window, and went to work.

Carefully breaking the hard crust away, he patted and kneaded and shaped the soggy inside of the loaf. Twice he slipped to the door and peered through the crack at the little derringer hanging on the wall. Finally he laid the result of his labors in a patch of sunlight and regarded it exultantly.

"Damn if she don't look enough like a gun to be one! Sun'll dry her hard in a little bit, too!"

Cracks appeared in the "gun" as the surface hardened. Ran carefully filled them with bits of moistened bread, shaping and smoothing them into place.

The sun sank behind the western mountains. The jagged peaks flamed crimson and gold and saffron and copper. Blue and purple shadows brimmed the canyons. Stars pricked through the sky like silver needle points in a black velvet robe. Lights glowed yellow. A guitar sobbed softly.

Ran heard the jailer come in, mumbling curses as he lit the lamp. Keys jingled. The outer door swung back.

"I bring you more beans," growled the jailer.

Ran stepped up after the pan had been shoved through and leaned against the bars.

"Say you want me to show you how that short gun works?" he asked softly.

The jailer gutteraled in his throat. "*Si*, but not tonight. Tomorrow will do. I——"

Ran's soft drawl broke in. "Won't be here to show you t'morrer, but here's its bunky you overlooked. I'm gonna show you how *it* works right now."

His slim bronzed hand whipped into view, holding the exact counterpart of the derringer hanging on the wall. The jailer gaped at the yawning black muzzle.

"*Madre de Dios!*" he breathed.

Ran's voice barked at him, edged with steel:

"Get them keys offen yore belt. Unlock this door, *pronto!* Make one funny move and I'll blow a hole through yore belly big enough for you to crawl through. Move!"

The jailer whimpered as he loosened the keys with trembling fingers.

"Have mercy, excellency!" he gulped. "I am a poor man with many children who will starve should I die."

"Look out you don't do somethin' to make them hungry, then," Ran warned him. "Pull 'er open!"

The door swung open. Ran stepped through, left hand swinging level with his knee. The hand whipped up and over. There was the sullen "chuck" of hard knuckles smashing against an unshaven jaw. Ran stepped over the jailer's body and jerked his gun belt from the wall.

He buckled the belt around him, thrust the derringer into a pocket and walked swiftly from the room. He slipped around the building and high-tailed it for the shed back of the jail. The gelding snorted a greeting. Ran rubbed the velvety nose that nuzzled his hand and cinched with lightning speed. He swung into the saddle and headed the black toward the main street.

Grim and ghastly, his torn face mottled with dried blood, his black hair matted with it, he rode to the *alcalde's* office. A moment later a bullet crashed through the window beside the mayor's desk.

There was a shout of alarm and the sound of

hurrying feet. Through the door burst the *alcalde*, face convulsed with rage.

The rage blanched to stark terror as his eyes rested upon the terrible face of vengeance glaring at him from the back of the tall black horse.

"*Sangre de Cristo!*" he gasped.

Ran Hollis leaned forward, lips drawn back from his white teeth.

Crash!

The *alcalde* screamed as the heavy bullet tore through his chest. He screamed again as the black horse spurned his writhing body with iron hoofs. Screaming and wallowing in the dust he died!

Out of the town, grim, terrible, rode Ran Hollis, into a land of myth and legend of his own making.

In the country of *Mejico* a story was born. A story that lengthened and grew. A story told in low voices around camp fires, breathed across the rangeland by wandering *vaqueros*, whispered with awe and wonder in the huts of the *peons*. A story and a name.

"*El Cascabel* rode in San Rosalee last night," mumbles a furtive laborer through the folds of his *serape*. "You recall the *alcalde* there? He who had Pedro and Miguel and Teresa, Miguel's wife, whipped until they died? He whips no more!"

"Now God in His mercy be praised!" comes the answering mumble. "He was a cruel one, that *alcalde!* Cruel also was the *jefe* at *Isidro*. Many men he hanged, for small cause. *He* will hang no more. *El Cascabel* rode also in *Isidro!*"

So the story went. The story of *El Cascabel*, The Rattlesnake, the rider in the night.

Alcaldes and other officers of *El Presidente*, who oppressed the *peons*, the humble people of the soil, learned to shudder at that name. Detachments of *rurales*, the efficient mounted police, were sent to capture the terrible lone rider. Soldiers marched with much noise and loud boasts; but *El Cascabel* rode where he willed and struck with deadly certainty.

"Lay your snares amid the mists of the mountain tops! Bait the traps with sunbeams of the dawn! Weave a net from star to star and walk with the wings of the winds! *Then* will you catch *El Cascabel*, perhaps!" derided the *peons* behind the backs of the frantic officials.

Chapter 3

EL AGUILA RANCH

FOUR men were busy near the mouth of a canyon. Busy with wooden pegs and strips of rawhide and a fifth man. There was also an ant hill and a jar of honey.

The four talked to the fifth as they pegged him down across the ant hill and smeared his face and hands with the honey. One of the talkers nursed a bullet-gashed arm. Another was solicitous of a knife wound that, had it been a couple of inches to the right, would have sliced his heart very neatly. As it was, the burn of it made him more than usually vicious.

"It will be the pleasure, indeed," he purred, "to watch while an ant runs into one eye socket and out the other, while you still live. It will be droll to listen to your screams, so long as you have a tongue with which to scream. Which will not be for long. A little more of the honey, Tomaso. Our little friends, the ants, they love it. *Ai*, they also love fresh blood. Perhaps it would be best that we slice off his nose and his lips and his ears before they begin. Your knife, Tomaso."

The man called Tomaso paid no attention to the request. He was gazing earnestly at a distant crest over which dipped a white ribbon of trail.

"Someone comes," he stated.

The others stepped away from the slender dark young man tied to the ant hill. They watched the approaching rider with narrowed eyes, hands close to the gun butts protruding from their holsters.

"*Gringo*," exclaimed one suddenly.

"It is so," said another, "*Americano*. What does he here?"

"It matters not," growled the leader of the band, a heavy faced man wearing much tarnished gilt upon his soiled government uniform. "He will ride on quickly if he knows what is well for him. That is," he added with an evil leer, "unless we judge it better that he remain with us for a while—it is a noble appearing animal that he bestrides."

The rider, tall and lean, with wide shoulders and a deeply bronzed face, quickly covered the distance to the group. A half-dozen paces distant he pulled his splendid black horse to a halt and sat regarding the scene before him with cold gray eyes. He spoke to the horse and rode a little closer.

No one of the four men saw just how he dismounted. One instant he was lounging with easy grace in the high saddle. The next he was on his feet, a tense hickory-and-steel figure of menace, slim, bronzed hands close to the black butts of the heavy Colts slung low on either thigh.

"What the hell's goin' on here?"

The voice that spoke the words was soft and drawling.

"*Senor,* what goes on here is no concern of yours. We are officers of *El Presidente.* We——"

"To hell with *El Presidente!*"

The stranger's voice was no longer soft. It was hard and brittle and edged with jagged ice.

The government men gaped in slack-jawed amazement. The prisoner, craning his neck away from the crawling ants, saw blood pulse redly through a great jagged scar extending from chin to cheek bone. A glad cry burst from his lips:

"*El Cascabel!*"

There was a moment of terrible silence; then the government men seemed to wilt and shrivel. They stared with fearful eyes at the dread figure of the tall man with the scar. There was hate, deadly and implacable, written on that bronzed, thin-lipped face. Just as plainly was frightful, ruthless efficiency written in the pose of the slim hands hovering over the black revolver butts. Death looked out from eyes gray and cold and utterly fearless.

For another awful moment Ran Hollis stared at the group. Then he gestured with his head—the tense hands never moved——

"Cut him loose!"

With trembling hands, the breath sobbing in his throat, the gold-braided leader obeyed. The prisoner staggered to his feet, beating and brushing the ants from his person. Ran gestured again, toward four horses grouped together.

"Ride!"

The prisoner found his voice:

"*Capitan*, they have my gun, my knife, my money—everything."

"Hold it," rasped Ran. "Shell out—turn yore pockets. Everythin'—you borrowed this feller's money. You can jest pay him a little int'rest. Knives, too, and guns. Fill up yore saddle bags, feller. Them horned toads is lucky they ain't fillin' coyotes' bellies. All right, you hyderphobia skunks, fork yore bronks and get goin', *pronto!*"

When the beat of hoofs had died away, Ran regarded the man he had rescued.

"Clean lookin' young feller," he decided. Aloud——

"How come they had you hawgtied, *hombre?*"

The other smeared the honey from his face and hands with a handkerchief as he replied.

"I gambled with them in Monica, ten miles to the north. I won. They grew angry and we fought. I wounded two and got away. But I was careless. I should have ridden from the town with great haste. There was a *senorita*, and—I lingered. They knew the route I would take when I rode from the town. They rode ahead and waited."

"I see," Ran nodded. "Now where you ridin'?"

"I ride back from whence I come," the *vaquero* said. "I ride to Silver River Valley."

"Silver River Valley," mused Ran. "Where's that?"

"In Sinaloa, *Capitan,* far to the south."

"Uh-huh. Well, you better get goin', 'fore them jiggers take a notion to get help and come back lookin' for you."

The young *vaquero* hesitated. *"Capitan,"* he said diffidently, "will not you ride with me? There is work in Silver River Valley for *El Cascabel."*

"What kinda work?"

"The work *El Cascabel* loves to do. There are wrongs to be righted, *Capitan.* The rancher for whom I ride will welcome you greatly."

For several minutes Ran pondered. "Things are gettin' sorta hot for me 'round hereabouts," he mused. "All the *rurales* in Sonora and mosta the army is out gunnin' for *El Cascabel.* They're liable to get a lucky break some time and then I'll be plumb outa luck. That's yore hoss over there under the tree, ain't it, feller? What's yore name?"

"Miguel, *Capitan."*

"All right, Mike. Fork yore bronk and let's ride."

South by west they rode, to where the mountains

of Sinaloa raked the brassy-blue sky with jagged fangs of stone. Where the ranches were of vaster extent, the cattle wilder and the ranchers more than ever like to feudal barons.

"The gate of Silver River Valley, *Capitan!*" Miguel exclaimed late one afternoon with dramatic abruptness.

Ran pulled to a halt and eyed the narrow, gloomy gorge which the trail they were following entered. A whitely foaming stream chafed one wall. Manzanita thickets shouldered the other. Less than half-a-mile distant the canyon curved sharply.

"How far does she run beyond that bulge?" he asked Miguel.

"Two miles—perhaps a little less, *Capitan;* then one enters Silver River Valley."

Ran spoke to the black horse. "All right; let's go"; he said, "if we're gonna get somewhere 'fore dark."

They entered the gorge, following a trail that zig-zagged along the bank of the stream. It wound and twisted like a snake in a cactus patch. The bulge of the bend loomed a few hundred yards distant.

Whe-e-e-e-e!

Ran ducked instinctively. The whinning bullet had literally fanned his face with the breath of its flight. Thin with distance, the crack of the rifle drifted down from somewhere amid the rambling cliffs. A multitude of rioting echoes made it impossible to locate the sniper from the sound. Ran crouched low on the black's neck and probed the threatening rocks with his glittering pale eyes.

Whe-e-e-e! Whop!

Miguel's horse screamed shrilly, reared high and went over backwards. The *vaquero* snaked himself out of the saddle barely in time. He came to his feet spitting gravel and curses in two languages. A third whining slug flipped a patch of hide from the rump of Ran's horse. The black gelding whirled about and bolted madly back the way he had come. A bullet had turned Ran's hat sideways on his head and another had cut the bridle half in two before the cowboy got the frantic bronk under control.

"C'mon, Mike!" he yelled. "Let's get outa this!"

Miguel leaped from behind a sheltering boulder and fled down the canyon. Ran got his cayuse's head around and raced to meet the *vaquero*.

The gorge was humming to a dull, ever loudening rumble. "What the hell?" Ran muttered. "Sounds like——"

Around the bend roared a nightmare vision of rolling wild eyes, crashing hoofs and tossing horns that filled the canyon from stream bank to beetling cliff wall. The thunder of the churning hoofs that beat the manzanita flat drowned Miguel's scream of despair.

As if he were standing still, the stampede rolled down upon the *vaquero*. The black horse wavered, snorting with terror. Ran grimly drove his spurs home and charged straight for the horror of those goring horns.

Miguel stumbled, floundered, went down. Ran swore between set teeth, leaned far over and gripped the *vaquero's* collar with slim, steely fingers. The black horse performed the utterly impossible feat of turning in mid stride at full speed.

With a mighty heave Ran hauled Miguel's slight form across the saddle in front of him. The gelding screamed as the hot breath of the stampede seared his flanks.

Ran jerked a gun and fired right and left at the maddened steers. A charging horn ripped his overalls from ankle to knee. Another gashed the gelding's haunch. The bellowing cattle surged away from the blazing gun and the gelding won free. He was half-a-mile away from the mouth of the gorge and the scattering herd before Ran could pull him to a halt.

Miguel dropped to the ground. Ran rolled a cigarette with steady fingers and eyed the dark mouth of the canyon.

"Mike, it looks like some sorta playful *hombres* hang out in there," he drawled.

Miguel said things that smelled of sulphur. "It is as always, *Capitan*," he concluded. "Thus is it ever with The Eagle Ranch. Our cattle are stampeded! Our *vaqueros* are murdered! Our barns and hay stacks are burned! *Maldito! Caramba! Cospita!*"

"Uh-huh," Ran nodded. "Don't blame you for cussin'. Question right now is, will them drygulchers still be waitin' for us if we ride back in that darn hole-in-the wall?"

Miguel shook his head decidedly. "Not so, *Capitan*. Ere now they will have slunk away like the coyotes they are. But we will find their handiwork before we have passed through the gate. Doubt not that, *Capitan!*"

They found the "handiwork," even as the *vaquero* had predicted—the bodies of two dark-faced young riders, shot in the back!

"Eagle *vaqueros*," said Miguel, "and that was an Eagle trail herd—I read the brands."

"But there should be others besides these two," he added. "*Don* Tomaso would never have sent the herd out with but two to guard it."

Ran was grimly regarding the murdered men. The jagged scar stood out darkly against the deep bronze of his face. His eyes gleamed coldly under their black brows. Miguel, remembering the stories he had heard of the man, breathed soundless words against the back of his teeth:

"*El Cascabel!* Now, *Don* Felipe, *Don* Arturo,

look you to God for help—man will avail you not at all!"

Ran glanced up. "Callate the rest of the herd riders got away," he told Miguel. "We'll soon run acrost them if they didn't."

There were no more bodies in the canyon. With fantastic abruptness it mouthed into a valley set like an emerald cup amid the sky-reaching mountains. For a long minute Ran sat gazing at its breath-taking beauty of green and gold and silver and blue.

"Full ten miles wide, I'd say," he estimated, "and about four times that long.

"What's the other side that big hill, Mike?" he asked aloud, nodding toward a huge mountain that reared its misty bulk across the south end of the valley.

"Another valley and more mountains, and then more valleys," replied the *vaquero*. "It is the trail to manana, *Capitan*."

"The trail to *tomorrow*," Ran translated. "Not a bad trail for a feller that rides from yesterday! Ever try to ride away from yesterday, Mike?"

"*Capitan*, I do not understand," replied the puzzled *vaquero*.

"Don't ever learn to," Ran told him briefly.

Through the sunset glow, the blue-purple dusk and the star burned night they rode a trail that swooped and tumbled across broken ground near the west wall of the valley.

"This is a hard road, *Capitan*," Miguel said, "but it is the best road for us. Here we will be safe against surprise and attack."

With the gelding carrying double, progress was necessarily slow. Dawn was flushing the eastern peaks with rose and saffron when the weary pair sighted the ranchhouse.

"At last," groaned Miguel thankfully. "Soon, *Capitan,* we shall eat, and rest. I famish, and I am of the great weariness."

Ran, gaunt and hollow-eyed from lack of sleep, chuckled mirthlessly.

"Uh-huh, my stomach's plumb decided my throat's been cut!"

As they clattered up to the wide veranda, a man came out and descended the steps. His legs moved in a queer jerking, halty manner that made his gait little better than a shamble. "Shore bad crippled," Ran mused.

"*Don* Tomaso," said Miguel, dropping to the ground as Ran pulled the gelding to a halt.

"Howdy, stranger. What the hell happened to yore hoss, Miguel?" said "*Don* Tomaso"!

Ran stared at the chunky, black-haired man who grinned up at him.

"Feller," he drawled, "you may get yoreself called a *Don*, but you shore marvericked that handle."

The crippled chuckled. "You plumb missed yore

throw that time, cowboy. I got jest as much right to it as any jigger whose grandma was the daughter of a *hidalgo*. Mine happened to be *La Senorita* Teresa Menendez, daughter of old *Don* Jose Menendez, 'fore she married Grandpa Simpson."

"The hell you say!"

"Uh-huh. But light down outa that hull. I'll have the cook rassle you some chuck. Miguel, you come along too after you tell a wrangler to look after that hoss."

Ran gave the cripple another keen scrutiny, and relinquished his bridle to the wrangler, although it was against his fixed custom to let another look after the gelding.

"Got the earmarks of a reg'lar jigger," was his silent comment as he followed the cripple into the big white ranchhouse. "Wonder what's the matter with his laigs?"

Ran found out as he surrounded a man-sized slab of crippled-cow, hot biscuits, native honey and other things.

"Tom Simpson's the handle," volunteered the cripple. "Yeah, I own the spread, what's left of it. Funny things been happenin' here since I took her over, 'bout a year ago. This crippled-crawler fashion of walkin' I puts on is one of the funny things. Bullet layin' 'longside my backbone—local sawbones is 'fraid to try and cut it out. Got it one evenin' when I was ridin' home from the nawth range. Drygulchers plugged me outa the hull and if Walt Dexter hadn't happened along 'bout the same time a couple *Don* Felipe's *vaqueros* come ridin' down outa the hills, I guess I'da been a goner."

"Who's Dexter and *Don* Felipe?" Ran asked.

"Dexter runs the ranch that lays to the east of mine. It's American owned—big boss lives in Arizona. *Don* Felipe Fuentes owns the big spread nawth of my Bar-A."

"What's all the trouble here?"

Simpson shrugged. "Mexicans, most of 'em, figger Grandma Teresa oughter left the ranch to somebody of the Menendez family. My pappy went to Arizona and married an American girl—so the Menendez blood runs mighty thin in me. They never had much use for Grandpa Simpson—proud lot, them old *Dons*. Figger if they run me out the ranch'll go back to somebody named Menendez, or somethin' like that. They damn near got it done!"

"Shore it's the *Dons* tryin' to run you out?"

"Hell! who else?"

Ran nodded. "Guess yuh're right."

For some minutes they ate in silence. Then Simpsom spoke again, diffidently.

"Up to the time I got this slug in the back, I was givin' 'em a purty good scrap. Now I can't ride wuth a *peso* and my hand shakes till I can't hold a gun straight. Feller, I'm shore up 'gainst it. If I could hold onto this here ranch—she'll pay big if she's handled right—I could get enough money t'gether to go back to the States and have a operation. They could cut that chunk of lead out in a good hospital and I'd be all right again."

The man's face was suddenly haggard and old, his eyes tortured.

"There's some other little things," he said. "Things what don't int'rest anybody else but are mighty important to me. Feller, with a little of the right kind of help I b'lieve I could scrap it out here."

"Uh-huh? What kinda help?"

Simpson leaned forward and laid a shaking hand on Ran's sleeve.

"If I had a foreman who could line my *vaqueros* up—they're a good lot—and not be scared out by *Don* Felipe and *Don* Arturo and the rest of 'em— but what's the use! Anybody signin' on here will be buckin' *El Presidente's* official crowd, too, and that's askin' too much."

Ran Hollis' eyes narrowed slightly, but he showed no emotion in voice or gesture. Only the jagged scar abruptly burned a dull, angry red.

"I'm needin' a job purty bad, feller," he said softly.

Simpson stared, incredulous.

"You—you mean you'll sign on with me? After what all I've told you?"

"Guess that's 'bout the size of it."

Simpson turned away, his face working, and

when he turned back to face the lean, somber cowboy, Ran Hollis did something he hadn't done in
many, many months—*he smiled!*

"You—you'll bunk here in the *casa*," Simpson
told him.

Chapter 4

ONE OF THE LITTLE THINGS

A GOOD range, the Bar-A, Ran quickly decided. The *vaqueros* were good men, too, although now thoroughly demoralized by the killings from ambush, the open threats, and the raiding that had been going on for months. Ran gave them a plain talking to:

"This outfit ain't gonna be kicked 'round any more," he said. "If there's any bootin' to be done in this valley, we'll do it. I'm backin' any play you make to the limit, and I'm lookin' for you to back me. Now I want a trail herd rounded up in a hurry —this ranch has got a contract it's gonna lose if we don't make a shipment *pronto*. And we need the money damn bad. Get goin'!"

The demoralized riders squared their shoulders and grinned. "Ha!" they said among themselves. "Miguel spoke truth when he said this new *capitan* was a hard one! Hard, *si*, but one a man may follow with confidence and without fear. Brothers, let us do as he says, and without delay!"

Cattle other than those bearing the Bar-A brand

watered at the stream running through the middle of the range. Ran asked Simpson about it.

"Bowtie—Dexter's outfit—ain't got no water to speak of. That's why Walt is so damn anxious to back me up in this scrap—if the *Dons* get their hands on the Bar-A, Walt is liable to be outa luck."

Ran stared at the misty cliffs walling the eastern side of the valley.

"Without Bar-A water the Bowtie jest ain't wuth a damn as a range," he commented.

"Uh-huh," agreed Simpson, "that's 'bout the size of it. Walt sits up nights worryin' 'bout what'll happen if I lose out here. He's been plaguin' the life outa his boss up nawth to get help for me."

Ran got his trail herd together, a big one, for cattle were plentiful on the Bar-A range, despite losses. Simpson shook his head pessimistically.

" 'Fraid you'll never get 'em to Laradeo, the railroad town," he said. "We tried it twict the last coupla months. You saw what happened the last time. 'Bout the same thing happened before, only closer to town."

Ran's thin lips tightened. "Somebody's liable to get a s'prise this time," he drawled.

They did, several somebodies!

The evening before the trail herd started for Laradeo, Miguel rode in, dusty and tired, but with his black eyes burning brightly.

"This I learned in the town, *Capitan*," he said, and whispered long and earnestly.

Ran issued brief orders and through the rustling dark a silent company rode from the Bar-A bunk-house, bearing long-barreled rifles and a burning desire to use them.

"Forget not *El Capitan's* instructions," Miguel cautioned his eager men. "Await the signal."

The trail herd started before sun-up. Late afternoon found it plodding its weary, bawling way between the frowning walls that formed the gate into Silver River Valley. Nothing had happened. Nothing happened now. The canyon remained silent save for the querulous grumble of the rushing river and the scrambling echoes the passing cattle kicked up. Ran, lounging loosely in the saddle, rode ahead, a single *vaquero* by his side. The *vaquero* hissed suddenly.

"Look, *Capitan!* Where the walls cease!"

Ran nodded. Even before the keen-eyed *vaquero* he had seen the silent group sitting their horses in the mouth of the gorge.

"Looks like the show's gonna open," he said briefly, and rode on.

"Halt where you are!"

The command rang out sharply as Ran approached within fifty yards of the waiting horsemen. Their leader, a huge swarthy man, rode forward a few paces.

"*Gringo!* Tell your dogs to turn this herd and take it back whence it came!" he thundered. "Yourself, ride to me, with your hands above your head!"

Ran's thin lips twitched slightly as he raised his hands high in the air. The twitch became a wolfish, mirthless grin as from behind the silent rocks flanking the canyon trail rose up lines of grim-faced Bar-A rifle-men, the late sunlight glinting redly on the barrels of their leveled weapons.

"Shall we fire at once, *Capitan?*" called Miguel, hopeful eagerness in his voice.

Ran shook his head and rode steadily toward the swarthy leader, whose men were milling together in a terror stricken huddle. The big man's face had paled slightly, but he faced the cowboy with sneering lips.

"Shoot, gringo!" he hissed. "You are a brave man—with many rifles at your back!"

Ran rode within a dozen paces of the other, and pulled up.

"Shuck off them hawglegs," he ordered quietly, "let yore belt drop on the ground. Then slide outa that hull. *Muy pronto!*"

Under the threat of the cowboy's pale eyes the big man obeyed, mumbling curses. Ran gazed at him speculatively.

"Sets up to be a salty *hombre,* eh?" he said, almost to himself. "Well, we'll jest see *how* salty."

His bronzed hands dropped to his own gunbelt,

loosened it quickly and passed it to the wondering *vaquero* who sat his horse beside him.

"Let me have that sticker of yores, Guillermo," he said.

The *vaquero* drew his heavy knife and handed it to Ran. "Assuredly, *Capitan,* here is the blade. Cut that one's throat quickly. Then will we shoot the others and be on our way. It grows late."

Ran chuckled as he swung to the ground. With a single quick gesture he ripped the silk handkerchief from about his neck.

"All right, *hombre,* let's see you back yore big talk up," he said. "Pull that frawg sticker outa yore belt and let's go to it."

Gripping one corner of the handkerchief between his teeth, he thrust the other at the big man. The other backed away, his face a pasty gray.

"I—I do not understand," he quavered.

From the watching riflemen lining the cliffs went up a yell of derision. What man of the land of *Mejico,* be he stately *Grandee* or humble *peon,* does not understand *el duello* of the knife? Where two brave men, gripping with set teeth the handkerchief that holds them together, fight breast to breast to the death. Even the huddled group, cowering under the threat of the rifles, gazed with eager eyes and bated breath. This was a scene to the liking of all.

Straight and tall and steely as a lance at rest, the cowboy stood, one slender bronzed hand gripping the heavy knife, the other extending the bit of gay silk; but the big Mexican gave back.

"If I won, your men would murder me!" he mumbled. *"No!* my orders are not thus!"

Quietly Ran looped the handkerchief back around his neck. He tossed the knife to Guillermo, who caught it deftly and thrust it back into its sheath. Ran took a long stride forward, his left hand lashed out, slapping the big man across the face, right and left, bitter stinging blows that sent him reeling back.

"Listen, you," said the cowboy, his voice cold, toneless, deadly, "go back to the feller what gives you orders and tell him I'm lookin' for him. Tell him when I find him I'm gonna shuck his hide off and ram it down his throat. And as for you, you yaller livered, crawlin' hyderphobia skunk! If ever I even see you again on this range I'm gonna drill so many holes through you you'll leak all yore vittles out and starve to death. Now get goin'!"

As the shivering group got under way, Miguel's disappointed wail echoed from the cliffs.

"Capitan! may not we fire now? It eas most uncomfortable waiting here during the night and the day. Just one bullet each, *Capitan!* Those that survive may go free."

Ran grinned thinly but shook his head.

Laradeo was more than a shipping town for the surrounding spreads, Ran learned. There were rich mines in the hills to the south. Men were drilling for oil at the edge of the desert that rolled, stark and forbidding, to the west. Laradeo was a booming, roaring hell-town, Mexican style. It resembled other boom towns Ran had known, but was different —different as a heavy chopping knife differs from a slim, silver-steel blade.

"Bet she howls after dark with the best of 'em, though," Ran told himself as he threaded his way through the busy mid-afternoon streets.

He completed his business with the shipping agent, received an urgent request for another and larger herd, and decided not to head back for the ranch immediately.

"You work dodgers been doin' purty well of late," he told the grinning *vaqueros*. "Guess you got a little vacation comin'. Go to it, and see how many of you can get busted haids 'fore mawnin'!"

The *vaqueros* "went to it," boasting between drinks of their *capitan*, who could "out-rope, out-ride and out-shoot any *capitan* in the state of Sinaloa, doubtless in all Mexico!"

The *capitan*, in the meantime, rustled some chuck and a few drinks in a better-class *cantina*. As he leaned against the bar, listening absently to the chatter of a friendly drink juggler, he noticed two men seated at a nearby table.

One, much the older, was a gentleman without a doubt—white-haired, stately, with a fine, intelligent face. The other, richly dressed as his companion, was much younger. He had a reckless, dissipated look.

"*Don* Felipe Fuentes and *Don* Arturo Menendez," whispered the bartender. "*Don* Felipe is a *Grandee*. *Don* Arturo—he is of good blood, but——"

An expressive shrug completed the comment.

Ran eyed the pair with interest. These, then, were the owners of the ranches to the north of the Bar-A—these were the men Tom Simpson suspected as being the trouble makers who were trying to run him off his ranch.

"Arturo looks like that kinda horned toad," Ran decided. "*Don* Felipe don't—but you can't go much by looks down here."

The loquacious bartender kept talking.

"*Don* Arturo is to marry *Don* Felipe's daughter, they say. Rosa, she is named, and truly is she a rose, but *Don* Arturo! *Senor*, it is the pity!"

When darkness fell Laradeo howled, all right. Ran began to really enjoy himself for the first time since leaving Arizona. It was hard to brush shoulders with these gay, laughing, roistering Mexicans and not become exhilirated. Mellow *mescal* and fiery *tequila* helped. So did the flashing dark eyes of the dance hall girls.

Ran drifted from *cantina* to *cantina*, having a drink, a whirl at roulette or monte. He danced with the vivid girls who chattered lilting Spanish at him so fast he could not understand the half of it. Several times he encountered one or more of his own men, evidently having the time of their lives.

As the night wore on, the atmosphere of *cantina* and dance hall grew more tense. The *pulque*, the *mescal* and the *tequila* were getting in their work. Blood began to mix with the liquor staining the bars. Knives glittered in the lamp light, curses were hissed, blows were struck. Ran loosened his guns in their sheaths and began paying more attention to what went on around him. After a time he drifted back to the big *cantina* in which he had seen *Don* Felipe and *Don* Arturo many hours before. Neither of the two was present.

Ran stood for some time at the bar, sipping a drink and watching the dancers. The proprietor, a chunky, pleasant-faced fellow who looked like he had more than a dash of Indian blood, sidled up alongside the puncher. He was evidently ill at ease.

"*Senor*," he said in a low voice, "I have a message —a message from a—a *senorita*. She wishes to see you."

Ran grinned down at him. "Uh-huh? *Senoritas* in these kinda places us'ally want to see fellers. Nice of her, but I'm jest a pore cowpoke what's been outa a job a long time. Tell her to wait till payday."

"*Senor*," protested the saloon keeper earnestly, "you misunderstand me. This *senorita* is—ah— different. She is most anxious to speak with you."

The grin left Ran's lips. The cold, watchful glitter of the hunted birthed deep in his pale eyes. There is, he well knew, no better bait for a man-trap than a woman.

"Where's this here *senorita?*" he asked the proprietor.

"Seated at the table just back of the guitar players," replied the other instantly. Reading the look in the cowboy's eyes aright, he added, "There is nothing amiss, *senor*, I assure you."

Ran arrived at a sudden decision. "All right," he said.

"She awaits you, *senor*."

Ran shrugged his shoulders and sauntered across the room. The table was in the shadow and he could make little of the girl seated there other than that she was small and slight, with a wealth of dark hair and great dark eyes.

"*Buenos dias, senorita,*" he greeted as he sat down opposite her.

"Yes, it is morning now, isn't it?" she replied in English with just a charming trace of an accent. Then before Ran could reply she leaned toward him.

"You are in grave danger," she said. "There are those in this town who hate you."

"Who, Ma'am?" asked Ran quietly.

"I can't tell you—I don't know myself—but I know you to be the friend of one who is dear to me, and ordered my servants to watch carefully. They brought me the word."

"Ma'am," said the bewildered puncher, "you mind tellin' me who you are?"

"I am Rosa Fuentes," replied the girl.

"Rose Fuentes! *Don* Felipe's——"

"Yes," she interrupted, "the daughter of *Don* Felipe Fuentes."

"But why—what——"

Even in the dim light Ran could see the color rise in her creamily olive cheeks. She lapsed into Spanish, speaking softly, haltingly.

"*Senor,* I know you. You are the *Senor* Hollis who is the friend to Tom—*Senor* Simpson. He— we—oh, can't you understand!"

Ran nodded. "Yeah, I think I can. I'm beginnin' to und'stand what Tom meant by them 'other little things.' So you ain't gonna marry *Don* Arturo after all?"

The girl's eyes flashed. "I certainly am not! My father desires it. He has forbidden Tom seeing me, but I'd marry Tom tomorrow, if he'd agree. He refuses to do so until he has gone back to America and had the operation that will make him well."

Tears filled the dark eyes. "He—he will not take the money I offer him—I have so much. If he only would! Then we would not have to wait!"

"Don't you worry!" Ran told her. "He'll soon

have plenty of his own. We're gonna make that ranch pay."

"Oh, I'm sure you will!" she exclaimed. "You— look! Those men by the door!"

A compact group had entered the *cantina*. They spread out, blocking the door, commanding the entire room.

" 'A huge man, swarthy, with evil eyes,' said my servant," the girl whispered. "Is not that such a one there in front?"

Ran, peering in the shade of his wide hat, nodded grimly. He had already recognized his late antagonist of the canyon mouth.

Rose Fuentes was whispering tensely:

"There is a door, here behind this grill. It is locked and barred and will take time to open. You cannot move without attracting attention. Nobody will notice me. Sit quietly and when I have the bars down I will call."

Before Ran could say a word she was gone, slipping out of her chair and gliding behind the grill without the slightest sound. Ran drew a deep breath.

"Tom Simpson, yore the luckiest hoss thief what ever ambled down the pike!" he declared wordlessly. "Ain't she a wonder!"

Then things began to happen.

The swarthy giant, sweeping the room with keen eyes, suddenly let out a yell. He died with the shout on his lips, Ran's two bullets lacing twin holes through his heart. His companions went for their guns and the *cantina* rocked and roared to the heavy reports.

Bullets drummed into the table top behind which Ran crouched. He was showered with splinters and bits of hot lead. His own sixes were streaming fire and smoke, spraying lead across the room like water from a hose. Yells, shrieks, the screams of terrified women and the crash of breaking glass added to the uproar. Through the pandemonium Rosa Fuentes' clear voice cut like a silver blade of sound.

"The door—it is open!"

Ran's left-hand six tipped up. He blasted two big hanging lamps from their fastenings and sent them jangling to the floor. Darkness swooped down, through which the blazing guns stabbed long lances of yellow flame. Ran ducked from behind the table top, rounded the grill and leaped for a paler patch of darkness. A warm little hand grasped his wrist.

"This way," panted the girl. "Straight down this street! Now around the corner! We'll be safe in a minute!"

The *cantina* behind them still breathed fire and smoke and outrageous noises. Ran chuckled as his companion paused before a gate set in a high wall.

"All over," he told her. "Them jiggers will be busy the rest of the night tiein' up busted heads and things.   Ma'am, you shore are ace-high, and then some!"

Rose Fuentes dimpled up at him.   "Don't tell Tom about this," she pleaded.   "He'd be wild.   I don't want to worry him.   And if my father knew! The daughter of *Don* Felipe Fuentes in a *cantina* after midnight!   The poor dear would never understand.   He'd consider himself disgraced."

She giggled impishly.   *"Buenos noches, Senor Hollis!"*

The gate clicked open, and she was gone.   Ran straightened his hat and sauntered down the street.

"Don Felipe may be a this-that-and-then-some," he mused, "but he shore knows how to pick 'em when it comes to daughters."

Chapter 5

THE LISTENING MAN

RAN and his men left Laradeo the following afternoon. The *vaqueros* were in a jubilant mood, although regretting having missed the row in the *cantina*.

"What a fight it must have been!" marvelled Miguel. "Two dead and others, doubtless, wounded. All but the two dead *ladrones* vanished from sight with great suddenness."

"And you say nobody knows them two jiggers?"

"At least no one will admit knowing them," amended Miguel. "Doubtless, *Capitan*, those are hired killers brought from the southern mountains. By whom? Who knows?"

Ran did not mention to Tom Simpson the part Rosa Fuentes played in the affair. "If she wants him to know about it, she'll tell him herself," the puncher reasoned.

That afternoon the Bar-A had a visitor. Ran watched him ride up to the house, a big man, nearly as tall and much heavier than the cowboy. His face was square and solid, with a hard mouth and keen black eyes. The eyes questioned Ran's face and shifted under the puncher's cold stare.

"Simpson to home?" he asked.

"Nope."

The stranger looked irritated. "I'm Walt Dexter from the Bowtie," he said. "Any idea where I can find Tom?"

Ran waved a hand toward the big main room. "You might wait in there for him. He'll be back most any time now. Jest went up to the corrals."

After Dexter had entered the house, Ran went to his own room on the second floor. He pulled a chair to the window and sat looking out, a slight furrow between his eyes.

"That jigger shore reminds me of somebody. Who in hell——"

Simpson rode up and entered the house. Ran could hear the rumble of voices in the living room below. Somebody opened a window and Dexter's voice came clearly to his ears.

"Jest the same I don't like his looks, Tom. That jasper's a killer. Look at them eyes, and his hands, and the way them two guns is slung. He's bad!"

Simpson's chuckle drifted through the window. "That's one of the reasons why I hired him. I figgered I needed somebody bad."

Ran Hollis stiffened in his chair. A forgotten cigarette burned toward his fingers.

"Don't see how you ever come to trust sich a lookin' *hombre* as that," Dexter growled.

"Well, Walt," Simpson replied, "I was sorta askin' myself that same little thing, and then—I saw him smile oncet."

Ran relaxed in his chair and the cigarette came slowly to his lips. Dexter's snort was eloquent.

"Smile! I didn't think that jasper knew how to smile. He ain't the smilin' kind—he's a *listenin' man!*"

"Listenin' man?"

"Uh-huh. All them killers is. Notice how he holds his head a little bit to one side? Listenin' for a dead man to whisper over his shoulder!"

Ran Hollis's head abruptly jerked to the front and he stared with cold, bitter eyes out the window; but as he stared he seemed to look into a room dim with acrid smelling smoke. Under the smoke lay three quiet forms! Other visions came—visions of men who screamed and writhed, and died!

"They had it comin' to them!" muttered the cowboy. "Ev'ry damn one of 'em!"

But as he stared into the grim past, his head turned slowly, almost imperceptibly—*until his left ear was slanted slightly over his left shoulder!*

Walt Dexter rode away from the *casa,* apparently in a bad temper. Early the following morning he was back, in a decidedly worse temper and cursing like a madman.

"Yeah, the big waterhole over on yore south range!" he shouted. "The one my dogies use, too. Pizened all to hell! Dozens of beefs stretched out stiff. Jim Walker rode over with a shovel to clean the hole out and found 'em. Damn them greasers —Menendez, old Fuentes and all of 'em!"

Simpson swore wearily. "Now if this ain't hell! Pizen in a waterhole!"

"What'd you do 'bout the hole?" Ran asked Dexter.

"What the hell was there to do?"

Ran gave him a look of disgust and headed for the bunkhouse.

"Miguel," he barked, "get posthole diggers, hammers, axes, wire. Don't forget staples."

Ran found more than two dozen dead steers around the waterhole. Twenty-three of them were Bar-A cattle.

"Bowtie got off easy," he growled. "What's that, Miguel?"

Miguel was pointing to a film of steel-gray, lustrous crystals where a rock jutted into the pool. Ran nodded. "Uh-huh, arsenic."

A little later Ran found something else. Tangled in a clump of grass was a short length of *gold watch chain*—a dozen or so flat links of peculiar workmanship. One of the end links was spread apart at the joint. He also found, nearby, the faint imprint of shod hoofs.

"Caught on somethin' and busted loose when he forked his bronk," the cowboy muttered. "I wouldn't be s'prised if this here tick-tock hawgtie gives some jigger lead pizenin'.'"

Ran found Simpson in a gloomy mood when he got in that night from fencing the waterhole.

"Rose told me 'bout runnin' inter you in town," he said briefly without preamble. "You un'stand how things is with us. I been meetin' her purty often and *Don* Felipe has caught onto it. Now he's got *vaqueros* watchin' ev'ry move she makes. Pore kid might jest as well be in jail."

Ran asked a question: "What sorta jigger is old Fuentes?"

"Seems to be a purty good sort. Proud as a Yaqui buck with a red shirt. Sets a heap of store by his ancestors, who settled this country and were top-notchers in the old country. Thinks Rosa hadn't oughter marry anybody but a real, honest-to-Pete Spanish-Mexican *Don*. Guess that's why he's in this fight to throw me outa here—though you'd never be able to get him to admit it. I can't for the life of me see how he ties up sich doin's with his high-falutin' notions of honor."

The scar on Ran's cheek suddenly flamed scarlet. "*Honor!*" he blazed. "The gang what runs things

in this country ain't got no notions of honor or anythin' else decent!"

Simpson stared at the door through which Ran
had strode with clicking high heels and jingling
spurs. "Whe-e-ew!" he whistled. "I wouldn't have
that jigger feel that-a-way 'bout me for all the beef
steers in *Mejico!*"

While Ran and Simpson were eating supper,
Walt Dexter came in.

"I heerd from up Nawth," he told Simpson.
"The Big Boss won't let me mix inter things here.
All he did was offer to buy the Bar-A."

"The hell he did!" exclaimed Simpson.

"Uh-huh. Figgered if you was pullin' out anyway, he'd take a chance on buckin' the greasers for
the water rights."

"What'd he offer?" Ran asked.

Dexter named an amount. Ran swore. "Hell,
that ain't a third what this spread's wuth."

"I know it ain't, but he won't give more with
things like they are. What you think 'bout it,
Tom?"

"Mebbe I'd better take it," said the owner
wearily. "Looks like ev'things goin' to hell anyway. I guess——"

"Tom," Ran interrupted earnestly, "I'm in favor
of hangin' on a while."

Dexter sneered. "Wanta hang onto yore job
long as you can, you mean!"

Ran turned to face the Bowtie foreman, and his pale eyes were like snow-blown ice. He spoke slowly and distinctly in dead, level tones:

"Dexter, *any* job I start I aims to finish—*any kind* of a job! Think that over when yore in the notion of makin' funny remarks."

Dexter's eyes shifted nervously and he fumbled with his hands. "You needn't be gettin' all hostile," he grumbled. "I didn't mean nothin'."

"Tom," pleaded Ran, "wait until after t'morrer 'fore decidin' anythin', will you?"

"All right," Simpson agreed. "Come back Thursday, Walt."

Dexter didn't look pleased, but he merely nodded. "I'll pay cash when the deed's signed," he said. "The Boss wrote I could do that."

Ran asked an idle question: "Who owns the Bowtie?"

"My cousin up in Arizona—Cal Taylor."

"Cal Taylor!"

"Uh-huh," said Dexter, not noticing the sudden blazing light in the cowboy's pale eyes. "Him and me is cousins—he was named after my dad. Looks a bit like me but's a heap older. Cal owns sev'ral spreads this side the Line. Owns a big mine in that new gold town, up home—Arivapa, they calls it—too.

"He damn nere cashed in 'bout a year ago," Dexter rambled on. "Tinhorn shot him through the shoulder. Card sharp was a whizzer with a gun and drilled two of Cal's riders plumb center. Cor'ner's jury said it was self-defense, but the card sharp wasn't there to hear 'bout it. He'd drifted, *pronto!* Cal's friends down here purty near caught up with him oncet, but he busted loose again and dropped outa sight."

For a long time that night Ran sat staring out the window. Vague suspicions tumbled about in his mind. He fingered the fragment of watch chain he had found by the poisoned waterhole, and remembered with regret that Walt Dexter's heavy, well-worn chain had stretched unbroken across the front of his vest.

"Jest the same, anythin' Cal Taylor is mixed up in is crooked," he growled. "He's wuss than the *Dons!*

"Sorta glad I can go back to Arizona if I take a notion and not be on the dodge for murder," he continued his thoughts.

The next morning Ran rode north through Silver River Valley. As *Don* Felipe Fuentes was preparing to take his mid-day *siesta*, his servant announced a visitor. *Don* Felipe received Ran Hollis with chill courtesy.

"To what am I indebted for this honor, *senor?*"

Ran's cold eyes traveled over the face and form of the old *grandee.* He nodded grudging approval.

"Looks like a reg'lar *hombre,* anyhow. Looks like a man who would stick up for his friends."

The *Don* looked puzzled, and indignant.

"I trust that I am, *senor.*"

"Uh-huh. Then mebbe we can get t'gether a bit. I come here to talk to you 'bout a friend of mine—Tom Simpson."

"*Senor!* You will kindly refrain from speaking that name in my presence!"

"I kindly will not! That's what I came here to talk to you 'bout, and yore gonna listen!"

"You dare to speak to me thus, in my own house!"

A light red as the scarlet scar on his cheek flickered in the tall cowboy's eyes:

"*Don* Felipe Fuentes, I'd dare talk to the Boss of the Big Range Hisself this way if I knowed He was wrong and I was right—and yore a damn long ways from bein' God! I'm gonna ask you a question, and I want a answer—jest why don't you want yore daughter to marry Tom Simpson?"

The old man's face turned purple, but by a prodigious effort of an iron will he managed to hold himself in.

"*Senor,* I—I do not know why I am permitting myself to even listen to that question, but because you are my guest though an uninvited one, I will answer——

"My daughter is the last of an ancient house. She is a Fuentes! The *Senor* Simpson is——"

"Honest and decent, ain't he?"

"I have never had reason to consider him otherwise. But that is beside the question. His grandfather was an adventurer, a nobody who married a woman for her money."

"How old was they when he married her?"

"She was eighteen, I believe. He a year or two older."

"How old when he died?"

"Nearing seventy-five, if I recall rightly. But what——"

"Hmmm! Lived with her nigh onto sixty years —for money!"

"You argue shrewdly," admitted *Don* Felipe. "But nevertheless he was a nobody, and the *Senor* Simpson is descended from him. My ancestors——"

"Ancestors, hell!" Ran blazed at him. "I know all 'bout yore ancestors. Tom Simpson told me. Told me how proud you are of 'em, what fine people they were—real fightin' men and women. It's a fine thing to have ancestors like that, all right. Fine to be so proud of 'em you almost bust when you speak of 'em."

"*Senor!* I——"

"You listen to me! You ain't no ancestor—yet! But the time's comin' when you *will* be. When they'll be other Fuentes in this big house—Fuentes that'll be mighty proud of the old-timers back behind you. Ever think what'll they say 'bout *you?*"

"*Senor*, they will say——"

"Oh, yeah!" Ran interrupted him again. "*I'll* tell you what they'll say if you don't change some of yore damn fool notions mighty quick! This is what they're gonna say——

"'*Don* Felipe? Oh, that old four-flusher! He's the *hombre* what made his daughter marry a *mescal* swiggin' pig what oughta have been rode outa the country on a rail. Hell! let's don't do any talkin' 'bout that old so-and-so!'"

"*Senor*, they would not dare!"

"Oh, mebbe they wouldn't say it out loud—nice folks don't—but they'd think it, feller, they'd think it! And chances are there'll be a pore little dull-eyed kid settin' over to one side wonderin' with the little bit o' brain he's got to wonder with why he ain't strong and quick and lively and happy like other kids. If he had sense enough to know why, he'd damn to hell the *ancestor* what give him a drunken, woman-chasin', *marihuana*-smokin' he-goat for a daddy. *Ancestors!* Yeah, you'll be a fine ancestor, you will!"

The Mexican, tough old fighter that he was, quailed before the cowboy's flaming eyes. His hands shook. He bowed his white head and a great sob shook him.

"*Senor*," he quavered brokenly, "I little thought that ever would a man talk thus to me—and live!"

Suddenly the fine old head came up. *Don* Felipe

Fuentes, descendant of the Spanish Conquerors, rose to his feet and met Ran Hollis eye to eye.

"*Senor,*" he said, his voice firm once more, "you have opened the eyes of a foolish, selfish old man!"

"Hell, now yore talkin' like a reg'lar, honest-to-Pete ancestor!" Ran applauded.

"I intend to be one," said *Don* Felipe grimly. "You will please request the *Senor* Simpson to ride here and confer with me at his earliest convenience.

"Pedro," he told the servant, "wine for the *Senor* Hollis, and notify *La Senorita* that we have a dinner guest."

Chapter 6

BLAZING GUNS

TOM SIMPSON was the most astonished man in seven states and five counties when Ran delivered *Don* Felipe's message.

"That's jest what he said," Ran insisted— "Come to see him *pronto!* The little lady was cryin' and laughin' at the same time when I left.

"And, Tom," he added a little later, "damned if I don't believe that old coot was tellin' me the truth when he swore him and his men didn't have nothin' to do with the trouble we been havin' heah. I'm wuss puzzled and mixed up than ever. He looked at that chunk of watch chain and said he never knew of a Mexican wearin' sich a lookin' bunch o' links. Said he thought it was American make."

"Mebbe Arturo or somebody is bringin' gun fighters down from the States," offered Simpson. "I wouldn't put it past him."

"Might be," admitted Ran. "I got a little idea of my own, but nev' mind that right now. You get goin' for *Don* Felipe's place. I'm ridin' to the south range and won't be back 'fore t'morrer."

Ran got back early the following afternoon and was decidedly surprised to find *Don* Felipe awaiting him.

"Since *Senor* Simpson did not see fit to visit me at once, I felt it might be better to come to him," said *Don* Felipe. "My daughter insisted that I should."

Ran stared at him with narrowing eyes. "You mean to say Tom didn't show up at yore place? He left here yest'day mawnin'."

"But where could he have gone?" demanded the bewildered *Grandee.*

Ran called a servant. "Manuel, didn't *Don* Tomaso ride from here yest'day?"

"Assuredly, *Capitan,*" replied the servant. "He rode with the *Senor* Dexter."

"You hear him tell Dexter anythin'?"

"*Si, Capitan.* They discussed his intended trip to *Don* Felipe's ranch."

The "little idea" that had been gnawing around in Ran's brain suddenly sat down and uncovered its face. The cowboy issued crisp, decisive orders:

"*Don* Felipe, you ride back to yore ranch on the chance of Tom showin' up there. Get all yore men out lookin' for him. Manuel, when Miguel and the *vaqueros* come in, tell them to hightail it for the Bowtie ranchhouse. I'll be there when they get there!"

The Bowtie ranchhouse, not so large as that of the Bar-A, was of a more modern design. The bunkhouse was some distance from the main building.

Ran walked straight in without knocking. A man was seated at a table, a sheaf of papers in his hands. He glanced up as the cowboy entered, the papers dropped from nerveless fingers.

The seated man's eyes fell before Ran's cold stare, his lips moved thickly.

The Bar-A foreman's drawling voice broke the silence.

"Kind of a surprise for both of us, eh, Cal?"

Cal Taylor, whom Ran had last seen prostrate on the floor of Monk Holliday's Arizona saloon, moistened his dry lips with his tongue and gulped. Words seemed forced from him unwillingly.

"Where—where did you come from?"

"What difference does it make? I'm here."

"What—what do you want?"

"Fust, I want to see that cousin of yores. Where is he?"

"He's around here some place. I'll call him."

Taylor raised his voice and shouted huskily. Walt Dexter entered the room.

"How's Tom?" he asked Ran.

"That's what I come over about. Seems you was the last man what seen anythin' of him."

"What you talkin' about, Hollis?" demanded Dexter.

"Well, you and Tom rode away t'gether, and that's the last anybody's heard of him."

"But hell, feller, I left him jest below the ranch-house, where the trail forks. He rode on down the crik and I crossed and struck this way for home. I don't know nothin' about him."

"Well," began Ran, "he———"

The words suddenly died on his lips. Walt Dexter burst into a volley of curses. "Them damn greasers again," he concluded. "Old Fuentes is in it, I'll bet my last white chip. He pulled the wool over yore eyes right, Hollis. Fixed up his little plan to have Tom ride down there alone. Him and his gang met Tom somewhere along the way and dry-gulched him, that's what."

"Think so, Walt?"

"Yeah, I do. Don't you?"

"Nope, I don't."

Ran's voice was level, toneless. His right hand fumbled with a shirt pocket.

"I didn't hardly know what to think a while back," he went on in the same monotonously level voice. "I shore was guessin'. Couldn't seem to get nowhere. Right now I'm thinkin' purty straight. I think I can name the jigger what's responsible for Tom's disappearin', the same jigger what's responsible for all the hell raisin' that's been goin' on in this valley."

"What you talkin' about?" Walt Dexter demanded. "Who you mean?"

"Who? I'll tell you who, Walt. The sidewinder what poisoned that waterhole the other day. The hyderphobia skunk what dropped *this* when he forked his bronk and didn't miss it soon enough to remember where he lost it or to go look for it. *This!*"

The hand that had been fumbling in the shirt pocket shot across the table and placed in front of Cal Taylor a *short length of gold chain.*

Instinctively, Taylor's hand flew to his own shirt front, to where a *rawhide string* was knotted to the *broken ends* of a watch chain stretching from one pocket to the other!

For an instant the room was silent as death. Then——

"Get him, Cal!" roared Walt Dexter. He clawed at his holster, his heavy Colt flashed out.

Ran Hollis drew and threw his gun underhand as a boy tosses a ball. His two shots blended in a single roaring report. The Bowtie foreman crumpled up.

Ran's right-hand gun stabbed at Taylor.

"Don'tcha make a move, Cal! Where's Tom Simpson? Quick! You got damn little time!"

There was death in the cowboy's voice. Taylor blanched.

"In that room there, he ain't hurt."

"Stand up! Walk around the table. Steady with them hands."

Ran flipped Taylor's gun from its holster and spun it under the table. "All right," he told the ranch owner, "open that door and get him out."

Taylor obeyed, fumbling a bunch of keys nervously. He flung open the door and stepped inside the small room. A single window, closed and heavily barred, admitted light. Ran could see a bound and gagged man on the bunk. It was Simpson.

"Cut him loose," the cowboy ordered. "Hurry up!"

Taylor worked over the prostrate man for a moment and Simpson swung his feet to the floor, clawing at the gag.

The crippled man could hardly stand, but he struggled erect and stumbled across the room. Taylor followed and Ran backed through the door, keeping a close watch on the Bowtie owner. They were in the main room when a step sounded on the veranda and a voice called.

"Anythin' wrong in there, Boss? We heard shots."

Ran leaped for Taylor, but he was too late.

"Help!" rang the rancher's voice. "Bring the boys! Hel——"

With a slashing blow of his gun barrel, Ran knocked him senseless into a corner and whirled as boots clattered in the hallway. The squat form of Jim Walker, one of Dexter's American riders, loomed in the doorway.

Ran shot and Walker reeled back, clutching at his shattered arm. A gun cracked and the bullet knocked Ran's hat spinning. Both of the puncher's guns let loose in a smashing roar. Men in the hall yelled wildly and fell over each other getting out of range. Ran gripped the unconscious Taylor by the collar and barked to Simpson: "Inter the other room, Tom! Too many windows to this one."

Simpson scrambled under the table for Taylor's six. He limped after Hollis and closed the heavy door, all but a crack. Ran dropped Taylor onto the couch and peered through the window. There was shouting outside.

"How many men did Dexter have?" he asked Simpson.

"Not more'n half a dozen, unless this here horned toad brought some with him. He's been here nearly a month, keepin' under cover and directin' things. Wanted to get the Bar-A for next to nothin'. Dexter circled nawth after he left me by the *casa* and drygulched me proper. They tried to get me to sign a deed. Gave me till t'night to think it over 'fore bein' cashed in. It was Dexter what shot me last year. He'da finished me, too, if *Don* Felipe's riders hadn't happened along when they did. Did you kill him?"

"If I didn't, some jigger with a spade is goin' to play a mighty mean trick on him 'fore long," Ran remarked.   "Look out!"

A bullet glanced from one of the window bars and whined across the room. The two men dodged a rain of falling glass. Simpson crouched low and peered through the door crack. Ran edged along the wall and flung two quick shots out the window at forms moving among the trees.

A storm of bullets followed, knocking what little glass was left to fragments and thudding solidly into the opposite wall.

Silence fell. Ran peered through the window but could see nothing. Simpson let out a yell:

"Feller, they've set the damn house afire! Smoke's jest bilin' in that door!"

Ran peered through the crack. A gray cloud was rolling in from the hall.

"Hey, you damn fools!" he roared. "We got yore boss in here. If you burn us, he burns too."

"Yeah?" came a voice. "Let him burn. Think we don't know he's dead? Yore goose'll soon be cooked, *hombre,* and that ain't no funny talk, either."

Ran stared at Simpson and the crippled man stared back.

"If I wasn't in the shape I am, mebbe we could make a run for it and shoot our way through," muttered the Bar-A owner. "Tell you what, Ran, we'll head for the door and I'll stop and give 'em hell while you keep on goin'.''

"Oh, yeah, that'll be fine, won't it? Well, you jest stand on yore right ear till I do that little thing. Say, this damn smoke's thick. We'll have to shut this door purty soon or get smothered."

Bullets began to stream through the shattered window. They glanced dangerously from the iron bars, carromed against the heavy wall timbers.

"Some jigger's got up high where he can shoot down on us," sputtered Simpson through a shower of splinters.

Ran craned his neck for a glimpse through the opening.

"In the bunkhouse. It stands on higher ground. Looks like the whole outfit's blazin' away through the windows. They can cover the front door from there, too."

Simpson swore as a screeching bullet burned his cheek. "We gotta plug that hole in the wall some way, feller!" he shouted.

"Mebbe we can stand the bunk up against it," Ran said— "nope, that's fastened to the wall. What's them boxes under it? One of them would jest fit against the bars."

Simpson hauled out one of the chunky boxes.

"Heavy as hell," he panted. "This'll be jest the thing."

He crouched beneath the window and slowly

shoved the box up along the wall toward the opening. It tipped against the bars. A bullet knocked a splinter from its edge. Ran gave a frenzied yell.

"Pull that thing back down, feller? Don't drop it! Hell's-fire-and——"

Simpson *did* drop it. Ran dived wildly forward, caught the box in mid air and sprawled on his face, the box held high in his outstretched hands. He placed it gently on the floor and rolled over to face the astounded Simpson. Wordless, he pointed to the red lettering stamped on the wood.

"Oh, my gosh!" gurgled Simpson. *"Dynamite!* That new powder what goes off when yuh jar it, and I was puttin' it up there for them sidewinders to throw lead at! Feller, there wouldn't been enough of us left to grease a gun barrel!"

Bullets were still coming through the window. The smoke was thicker and it was getting hot. Ran crept to the door, peered through the crack. He could see only swirling gray clouds. His straining ears caught no sound other than the crackling of the flames.

"The whole damn gang's there in the bunkhouse, shore as yore a foot high," he told Simpson.

"Can't we make a run for it?" coughed the crippled man.

"Not a chance; they'd drop us 'fore we'd gone a hundred feet. That's why they're in there—so's they can plug us and be under cover themselves. Lemme think a minute."

He stared at the dynamite box with bloodshot eyes. "Gimme yore knife," he exclaimed suddenly.

He shoved the heavy blade under the box top, pried it up and ripped it off, exposing the greasy cylinders. He dived under the bunk, shuffled about a bit and came out dragging another box.

"Caps and fuse," he panted. "Figgered they oughta be there. Help me fix some sticks for shootin'."

He worked swiftly, fastening a detonator and a short length of fuse to one of the cylinders. He gathered sticks together—six or seven of them— and tied them with his handkerchief, the capped and fused one in the middle. Then he stood up, face grim, eyes pale and cold.

"Trail after me," he told Simpson, "but don't come too fast."

He was gone before the other could say a word, vanishing through the smoke clouds. Cursing insanely, Simpson scrambled to his feet and shuffled after him.

Ran found the outer hallway heaped with burning brush. The walls were not yet afire. He dashed through the smolder, paused just long enough to thrust the fuse end against a glowing brand, and leaped down the veranda steps.

From the bunkhouse came yells and shots. Bullets whistled about the cowboy. The six in his own left hand streamed fire, flinging lead through the bunkhouse door and windows.

Straight for the bunkhouse he sped, weaving and ducking. The excited men there shot madly without taking time to aim.

Ran reached the bunkhouse wall unharmed. He crouched against it, close to the open door. He held the bundle of dynamite with its sputtering fuse before the opening, winced as some unthinking *hombre* sent a bullet zipping past it. His voice rose in a yell that drowned all other sounds.

"Drop yore guns and come out, every damned one of you! These devil-sticks is gonna let go in another minute and when they do we're all goin' to hell t'gether. Pluggin' me won't help a bit. Move fast, you sidewinders!"

There was a moment of stunned silence, then a clatter of falling hardware within the bunkhouse. Men spewed through the open door like seeds from a squeezed lemon, hands high in the air.

"Stop!" yelled Ran, "That's far enough! Hold yore gun on 'em, Tom!"

Simpson obeyed. The Bowtie riders milled together, casting frightened glances over their shoulders.

"Cut that fuse, feller," wailed one. "I'm too young to die!"

Ran reached for Simpson's knife, and realized

with a cold chill that he had left it in the ranch-house. He seized the fuse between his teeth, close to the cap, and chewed frantically. His teeth ripped through the outer covering. A gush of stinging sparks seared the roof of his mouth. The fire was already lapping against the cap! He leaped back a pace and hurled the bundle over the bunkhouse roof.

There was a terrific roar. The ranchhouse windows flew to fragments. The bunkhouse dissolved in splintered ruin. Every man in the yard was hurled headlong by the hurricane blast of the explosion.

Dazed and deafened, Ran weaved to his feet. His gun was still in his hand, but there was no need of it. Several of the Bowtie riders were unconscious, the others in no shape to offer resistance. Simpson was sprawled against the veranda steps, unhurt.

To Ran's numbed ears came a faint clatter of approaching hoofs. He tensed, then relaxed with a sigh of relief.

Into the ranchhouse yard swept Miguel and the Bar-A *vaqueros*.

"We come, *Capitan, muy pronto*. Manuel he tell us your orders when we arrive at the ranch-house. It has happened here what?"

"Never mind that, now," Ran told him. "Get that fire out fust thing and then take charge of them sidewinders on the ground. You all right, Tom?"

The *vaqueros* rushed into the *casa*. A tremen-

dous banging and stamping followed, and the hiss
of water on hot embers. The smoke thinned and
Miguel strode out again, his white teeth showing in
a grin.

"The walls he do not yet catch, *Capitan;* only
some holes in the floor. What shall we do with
these *ladrones?* Two are dead."

"Oh, let the live ones bury the dead ones," Ran
decided. "Then tell 'em to make themselves scarce.
They're jest hired men. Bring what's left of Dexter
out, too."

They found Taylor sitting up, looking pretty sick.
Ran regarded him coldly.

"Climb onto yore feet, and do some listenin'," he
ordered. The ranch owner obeyed, leaning heavily
against the table.

"A while back you told Dexter to make Tom an
offer for his ranch, didn't you?" Ran asked. Taylor nodded surlily.

"Got the money here to pay for it?"

"Yeah, I have. What of it?"

"Well, I been doin' a little figgerin'. What you
offered is jest about what the damage you did to
the outfit would come to. We'll jest take that
money and call it square."

"Like hell you will! Why you——"

"Listen, Cal," Ran interrupted, his voice coldly
brittle. "You bungled the job on me there in Arizona. You figgered on killin' me. You didn't do

that; but what you *did* do was make a killer outa *me!* That road runner of yores they jest drug out made about a dozen, Cal. I ain't a bit backward 'bout makin' it one more."

One of the long guns slid out, the single action clicked back, the black muzzle yawned at Taylor. Ran's voice bit at him like grinding steel:

"I'm goin' to count three. Make up yore mind quick. One—two——"

"Wait—wait—I'll do it! Damn you! Don't look at me like that!"

Taylor reeled back from the cowboy's terrible eyes, flinging up a hand before his face. He staggered around the table, sat down and opened a drawer. He pulled out a fat wallet and began counting money.

Ran checked the pile of large bills and nodded when the tally was complete.

Taylor snarled up at him like a rat.

"I'll get you for this some day, Hollis!"

"I'll be there at the gettin'. Now the best thing for you to do is sell Tom the Bowtie, at his own terms. The range ain't no good without Bar-A water. Then you'd better head for Arizona. Won't be healthy for you down here once this yarn gets out."

Nearly a month later, Ran Hollis sat in the Bar-A *casa* and read again a letter he had just received. His eyes lingered on the final paragraph:

"Outa the hospital and feeling fine. Rose and me'll be home next week and then we'll thank you right for all you did for us."

Том.

Ran folded the letter and frowned slightly. Somehow, he didn't want to be thanked for what he had done. He glanced about the room, his face cleared and he chuckled whimsically.

After all, his work here was finished. Tom wouldn't need a foreman now that he was well and strong once more.

Ran walked to the veranda and gazed south toward the misty mountain. Then he turned and gazed north toward where the white trail shimmered away in the moonlight. He thought of the dark, lithe men who had ridden with him up there in Sonora—*El Cascabel's bandidos*—and a smile quirked the corners of his wide mouth. Yeah, the boys would be glad to see him again. His thoughts leaped on farther north, toward the clean land of mountains and deserts and rivers and rolling range, and the lean, humorous men who hustled the dogies along with sweat and jest and rollicking song. A sudden wave of homesickness swept over him and with it a quickening heartbeat of gladness when he remembered that he had a clean slate up there now; that he could go *home!*

"B'lieve I will," he chuckled. "B'lieve I'll jest work my way up through Arizona sorta Nevada way, where Walt Stevens said that sidewinder Taylor owned his big mine. Lessee, Ari—Ari—uh-huh, that's it—Arivapa. Arivapa, Nevada. Sounds int'restin', somehow, and there oughta be lots of int'restin' things along the way—lots of hills with other sides, for instance."

He glanced north again. The trail shone white!

Working swiftly and efficiently, he hauled out his well-worn blanket roll. He placed a parcel of food beside the battered fryingpan and the smoky little coffeepot in the saddlebags. He wrote a few words on a sheet of paper and weighted it on the table in plain view. Then he went out and saddled up the magnificent golden sorrel that was a present from *Don* Felipe Fuentes.

The great horse snorted gaily and nipped his master's ear with velvet lips. Ran strode to the bunkhouse and aroused Miguel. The two men talked earnestly for a few minutes, and shook hands.

"It is with sorrow that I see you depart, *Capitan*," said the *vaquero*. "There will be heavy hearts here tomorrow."

Ran swung into the saddle, smiled down at the Mexican.

"*Hasta luego*, Miguel."

"*Adios, Capitan. Hasta luego.*"

Silently the *vaquero* watched the tall figure dim mistily away along the moonlit trail. "*El Casca-*

bell!" he murmured. "He rides from yesterday to tomorrow. May the sun for him rise brightly!"

He smiled wistfully as a deep voice drifted back to him in the words of an old cowboy song:

> "June along, hoss, we're goin' up a hill!
> June along, hoss, and don't stand still!
> When we find a hill what ain't got no other side,
> I'll do the junin', hoss, and you kin ride!"

Chapter 7

SAN SALVADOR

DUST and sun!

Dust and sun, and desolation! Clapboard shacks, warped, blistered by heat. Scoured and polished by the whispering sands that whirl fantastically in the grip of hot winds wailing under the blazing Arizona stars. Scrawny, listless men with bleached hair and leathery skins. A few discouraged women, eyes lacklustre with the ashes of burned-out dreams. Scabby dogs and gaunt horses. Now and then a stringy herd of wild-eyed cattle bawl-bellerin' to the shipping pens.

That was San Salvador, with its background of majestic mountains and the sun-golden, moon-silvered desert for a front yard. Study in shiftlessness and frustration.

And then——

A wild-eyed horseman lashing his lathered pony, whooping like a Yaqui buck full of squirrel juice, brandishing a buckskin sack. Into the single slatternly saloon he spurs his foaming horse, crashing through the swinging doors, scattering the cursing loafers. He yeols—a high-pitched, screeching squall, leans over and bangs the sack on the bar.

"Gold!" he bellows. "Gold in the Coronado Hills! Tons of it! Slathers of it! It's the Mother Lode, sho' as hell!"

The buckskin sack bursts open. Out tumble nuggets, rock vined and crawling with wire-gold, heavy dust.

"Drinks for the house!" bawls the rider. "Heah, barkeep, have a handful! I got plenty more! and theah's more wheah this come from! Boys, she's bigger'n Forty-nine, bigger'n Californy! Who-o-oppeeee! I'm a big he-wolf from Bitter Creek, and it's my night to howl!"

"Gold! Gold! Yellow gold!
Hard to get and harder to hold!"

Gold it was! Back in the Coronado hills was a stretch of meadowland in the shadow of a mighty mountain. It was, apparently, just like any other meadowland; but underneath the skin of earth in which flowers and grasses grew was a sponge of rock, and that sponge of rock was seamed and veined and shot with gold. It was the fabled "mother lode" which miners had sought since the days of Forty-nine.

Dust and sun! That was still San Salvador; but now it was the dust of roaring, thundering toil. The sun glared down upon life running red as the pulse

of blood from a severed artery. Clapboard shacks
were replaced by brick fronts. The lethargic inhabi-
tants gave way to bearded giants who ripped the
treasure of the hills to ribbons and in wild abandon
flung the gold salty with the sweat of utter toil to
the winds of romance, lust and mad desire. San
Salvador roared and thundered under the blazing
sun and the blazing stars. Red dawn was golden
noon before the clock hands had time to whirl
around. The blue dusk of evening was beaten back
by the brassy blare of lights that flamed and flickered in saloon, dance hall, gambling hell and pleasure
parlor. Miners in corduroys and blue woolen shirts
rubbed shoulders with gamblers in broadcloth, velvet clad Mexicans and cowboys in woolly chaps.
Indians stalked along the crowded streets, faces dark
above the flaunting red and brilliant blue of their
blankets. Women whose lips were too red and eyes
too bright went their silken way from shop to shop
to spend the gold that brawny miners poured into
their slim hands. At night when the lights blazed,
their short skirts swirled and billowed over the dance
floors or brushed against muddy boots where the
long bars were lined three deep. Spilled whiskey
and spilled blood soaked the sawdust in the saloons
and stained the cards at the gambling tables. Steel
flashed under the lights. Wisps of powder smoke
curled up to dim them. The roar of blazing guns
was drowned by the roar of drunken song. The

gurgling death yell might as well have died on the lips that died soon after, for all the sound was heard or heeded in the turmoil. Life's sands ran quickly through the glass, but they ran with a glow and glitter and a madness-bright sparkle.

Dust and sun! And gold and gunsmoke and adventure and romance! Passion and hate and love and lust.

That was San Salvador after the excitement-drunk miner spurred his foaming horse along the crooked main street and yelled his message of hills bursting with treasure.

South of San Salvador was rangeland. In the sheltered valleys the succulent gramma-grass grew belly deep. It was rich food for cattle when it waved, pale blue-green, in spring and summer. It was even richer when, in fall and winter, it was a golden brown. No need to cut and store hay in those valleys where the snow fall was light and the wind tempered by the surrounding hills.

The gold strike boomed the cattle business, for men must eat and ripping up sponge-rock makes for healthy appetites. But, there was a catch to it! The gold strike also emptied the bunkhouses. Wages rose fabulously, but riders to draw them were few. Only those in whose blood the lure of horse flesh and reeking leather and pounding hoofs ran strong clung to the range. The others abandoned chaps for corduroy and the silken rope for a pick handle.

The ranch owners found themselves in the position of a man who sees a feast spread before him but lacks teeth with which to enjoy it.

Into this seethe of unrest and irritation and thwarted ambition rode Bruce Belton. Behind him cantered hard-faced riders who wore their hair long and their holsters short.

"Belton was one of Quantrell's lieutenants," whispered the wise ones. "His men rode with Quantrell's raiders."

So said men who had known the ruthless guerilla leader. Belton and his men certainly looked and acted the part.

With Belton rode his niece, Ray Carrol, the only thing the widowed, childless Belton loved. Then there was Cale Winters, tall, dark, unbelievably handsome, who also called Belton "uncle."

Ray Carrol was more like a sun-kissed flower loose from its stem than anything else. Her hair was the color of a forest pool brimful of sunset, her eyes were blue, her lips like fresh roses. She was small and slender and born to laughter. She was range bred and could ride anything that walked on four feet.

Belton was a cattleman, shrewd and farsighted. He realized that gold strikes came and gold strikes went, but that cattle were in the land to stay. In this strike he saw opportunity.

He quickly acquired a couple of big ranches and

went into business. His men, who also recognized opportunity when they saw it, were not tempted by picks and shovels. With unguarded ranches all about plentifully stocked with prime dogies, why should they bend their backs over stubborn rock? There were easy pickings ready to hand for men of easy conscience.

All of which did not tend to improve old Wade Harley's temper. Harley's big range was well stocked with cattle, but his big bunkhouse was deserted. Also his cattle were disappearing at an alarming rate. Old Wade had his suspicions, but no proof. There had been no rustling of any moment on the Coronado range until after Bruce Belton rebuilt the Lazy-B ranchhouse and filled it with the furnishings a string of covered wagons brought across the prairie from the east. It might be merely coincidence, but——!

Growling under his breath, old Wade headed for San Salvador on the faint chance of picking up a stray puncher or two.

Chapter 8

RED-HAIRED ANGEL

RAN HOLLIS rode forth from Mexico. He rode fast and he rode alone. But he had "company"! Company that earnestly endeavored to make his closer acquaintance. Not that Ran was altogether a stranger to the dark-faced gentlemen in gaudy uniforms who clung so tenaciously to his wake.

With their fresher horses they steadily gained on him and when Ran's big golden sorrel flashed over the Line into Arizona, the pursuers had him in sight. With the quarry almost in reach of their vengeful guns, they paid not the least attention to international boundaries. Ran had not expected that they would.

The sorrel was giving everything that was in him, but he had travelled many, many miles and even *his* iron strength was failing. Ran began to anxiously scan the country ahead for some gorge or canyon in which he could make a last stand.

There was none in sight. For miles the slightly rolling desert and prairie land stretched unbroken, affording no concealment. To the north and west, misty with distance, loomed purple hills with the white-crested spires of mountains behind them.

"Might as well be the other side the sunset, for all the good they'll do me," growled Ran, loosening his guns in their sheaths.

On and on thundered the sorrel. He fled like the shadow of a star before a lightning flash, but still the grim-faced pursuers closed the distance.

And on a little covered rise, an unseen rider of a chunky pinto pony watched the uneven race through a pair of field glasses.

Suddenly the glasses snapped into their case and the pinto, obedient to a sharply spoken word, sped down the gentle slope.

Cr-r-r-rack!

Ran ducked instinctively. The crackling, splitting sound a high-power rifle bullet makes as it bores a hole through the air close to one's head is not pleasant to hear. Thin with distance, came the whiplash snap of the report.

That one was close, but the next one came closer. Ran actually felt the wind of it. He snugged low against the sorrel's neck and urged him on. Bullets were dropping all about, thudding into the ground, kicking up puffs of dust. The still faint sound of savage yells reached the fugitive.

On and on, with the hills looming closer and the

hoof-beats of the pursuit plainly audible. Ran twisted in his saddle and glanced back. He was tempted to try a shot or two but feared to do anything that might cause the sorrel to break his stride.

Suddenly the sorrel did break his stride. He broke it in an appalling manner. Heels over head he went like a shot rabbit. He struck on his back yards distant from the badger hole that had been his undoing. By a miracle neither his leg nor his spine were broken.

Neither was Ran's neck, although he landed partly on it when he was hurled from the saddle like a stone from a sling. Sick, dizzy, blood seeping from between his tight lips, he rolled over on his side and pulled his guns. The vengeful Mexicans, yelling like fiends, were thundering toward him. He could feel the wind of their bullets as they fired wild volleys without taking time to aim.

Ran did take aim and bruised, shaken and half blind as he was, he did damage. A man yelled shrilly and slumped onto his horse's neck. Another spun to the ground without a sound. A horse was hit and screamed its pain and rage. Ran shook his whirling head and pulled trigger as fast as he could.

Ominous clicks on empty cartridges warned him, but too late. He knew he would never be able to reload in time. They would be all over him in another moment.

The thud of hoofs behind him sent him twisting around. Surrounded! That did finish it!

Crash! crash! crash!

A rifle blazed directly over him. He stiffened for the shock of the tearing lead. The gun roared again before he realized that the shots were not for him.

From the pursuers burst wilder yells. The rolling beat of the hoofs broke raggedly.

But they were fighters, those dark men from below the Line. On they came in the face of the withering rifle fire. Two more saddles were emptied, but the remaining eight or ten charged madly across the prairie.

Ran, frantically reloading with fingers that seemed numb and useless, saw a slim figure drop from a plunging horse and crouch directly in front of him, shielding him from the bullets of the pursuers. He heard the rifle speak again and an answering yell of pain.

With a mighty gathering together of his strength, he rolled to one side and struggled to his knees. Up came the big Colts, steady as rocks. Coldly gray-green eyes glinted back of the sights. The black muzzles spouted flame and smoke.

The pursuing Mexican *rurales* were tough *hombres*, but there was a limit to what they could stand. This "coming to life" on the part of the man they thought they had downed was too much for them.

They wheeled their horses and galloped back the way they had come. With cool bravery and consummate horsemanship, they scooped up three wounded men and took them along with them. The dead they left where they were.

Ran Hollis tried to stand, but the iron efforts of the will that had held him up suddenly crumpled. He sank forward to lie in a huddled heap.

He came to with his head pillowed in a soft lap and the biggest and bluest eyes in the world looking down into his. Above the eyes was a white forehead and a wind-touseled glory of red curls. Below the eyes was a straight little nose delicately powdered with a freckle or two, a red, red mouth and an adorable little white chin.

"Guess I'm dead, all right," sighed Ran, closing his eyes.

"Dead!" exclaimed the girl in a startled voice. "Why—why——"

"Yeah," interrupted Ran, opening his eyes again, "I must be. I was allus told the angels stayed in Heaven. Only I never figgered a cowpoke had much chancet of gettin' there," he added.

The girl dimpled down at him.

"Thanks for the compliment," she said, "but whoever heard of a red-haired angel! You're a long way from Heaven yet, cowboy."

"If you hadn't happened along jest when you did,

I'da sho' got there, or some place, in a hurry. Wheah'd you come from, Ma'am?"

"I was watching from the grove over yonder. I could see that they were Mexicans and you were American. Also, ten or twelve against one didn't seem fair odds."

"You shore did even 'em up!" declared Ran with feeling. "You and that whole territory-full of nerve you pack along with you! Ma'am, if you'll 'scuse me for sayin' it, yore shore a wonder!"

Under the intensity of his gaze, the girl blushed. She changed the subject.

"Why were they chasing you?" she asked.

Ran's lean jaw tightened a trifle.

"Jest a little puhsonal matter," he replied.

He got to his feet, a little unsteadily.

"Can you ride?" the girl asked.

"Shore," Ran assured her. "I'm all right now— jest bumped my head a bit."

He examined the sorrel and was thankful to find he was not lamed. The girl, slim and graceful, had mounted her pinto.

"I'm headin' for a new minin' town I was told about, San Salvador," Ran explained as he swung into the saddle. "You ridin' that way, Ma'am?"

"No," she replied. "I ride in the opposite direction and I must hurry. My uncle is waiting for me at his ranch. *Adios!*"

"Say," Ran called as she wheeled the pony, "I ain't had a chance to thank you right for what you did for me. When am I gonna see you again?"

"Sometime—maybe!" she laughed over her shoulder. *"Adios!"*

Chapter 9

FISTS AND BULLETS

RAN HOLLIS rode into San Salvador. He rode a magnificent sorrel gelding. His riding gear, although not new, was costly. He wore a regulation cowboy outfit—overalls, chaps, dark shirt with handkerchief looped at the throat and a broad-brimmed "J.B." A well worn cartridge belt snugged about his lean waist. The plain walnut grips of heavy Colts protruded from the cut-out quick-draw holsters. Ran had exactly one silver dollar in his pockets. He had nothing in his stomach. He glanced longingly at a restaurant and sniffed his appreciation of the savory smells drifting through the open door. He turned into a side street where a livery stable sign creaked in the wind.

The silver dollar changed hands. The sorrel put on the nosebag. Ran tightened his belt a notch and strolled along San Salvador's new main street.

"She shore has got all the earmarks of bein' a salty *pueblo*," he nodded. "Guess they musta told us right down in *manana* land. I rode up heah from

Mejico lookin' for peace and quiet. I'm sorta gettin' a notion I didn't come to the right place."

He chuckled as a belligerent yell soared up from across the street, and entered a saloon, stooping slightly so that his hat crown would not strike the lintel of the door. It was early and the place was not yet crowded. Ran glanced about thoughtfully, his cold gaze coming to rest on two men who were arguing in front of the bar.

One was a wizened little old fellow with kindly blue eyes that were now blazing with indignation. The other, tall, broad-shouldered and astonishingly handsome, with clean-cut features, intolerent eyes and a mop of iron-gray hair, seemed more amused than angry.

"Yore talkin' through yore hat, Harley!" he jeered. "Chances are you jest can't count straight; but if you really have been losin' beefs, they must be goin' south. The border's closet to yore place and them greasers are mighty cute when it comes to wide-loopin'."

"I know others what are a darn sight cuter," growled old Wade Harley. "Belton, I tell you to yore teeth, yore men are rustlin' my stock, even if you don't know about it, and I ain't at all shore you don't!"

Bruce Belton's face flushed darkly.

"That's jest about the same as callin' me a liar and a thief, ain't it?" he asked quietly.

Old Wade met the hot glare of the intolerant black eyes sturdily.

"That's how I feel about it, Belton!" he replied.

Smack!

Belton's big hand, palm-open, lashed out and caught Harley side-of-the-head. It knocked the old man spinning. With a yell of anger, Harley came charging back.

This time Belton used his fist and Harley went down in a bloody heap. He staggered erect and headed for Belton a third time.

Ran Hollis reached out a long arm and gripped Harley's shoulder. He easily held him despite his struggles.

"Hold it, old-timer," he advised, "yore out of yore class."

"Lemme at him!" yammered old Wade. "I'll show the yaller cattle thief! I'll——"

"Uh-huh," demurred Ran. "Yore buckin' a losin' game. Theah ain't no sense in that!"

"Lemme go!"

"Turn him loose," said Belton. "He asked for it and he's got it comin'. I'd like to make a finish job of it!"

Ran regarded him coldly, still holding old Wade helpless.

"I don't see as yore gainin' much credit outa knockin' down a old man fifty pounds lighter'n you."

"What the hell bus'ness is it of yourn?"

Ran's soft drawl took on a metallic edge:

"I allus figgered it's any decent man's bus'ness to stop a hyderphobia skunk from fangin'."

With a wordless roar, Belton rushed. Ran flung old Wade aside and hit Belton, right and left, his fists slamming against the big man's jaw like a butcher's cleaver on a side of beef. Belton landed on his back with a crash that shook the building.

"Better stay theah," Ran advised. "It's safer."

Belton didn't stay. He came to his feet like a cat, blood dribbling from the corners of his mouth. He rushed again, arms flailing. Ran Hollis weaved aside, measured his man with cold gray eyes and let one go that started from the floor. It caught Belton squarely on the angle of the jaw. He halted in mid stride, spun around and went down on his face. He stayed there, skyrockets and pin-wheels exploding in his brain. Ran stepped forward and then went reeling against the bar as old Wade's shoulder caught him in the ribs.

Crash!

Ran heard the bullet yell past, felt its breath fan his cheek. He slewed sideways, guns coming out.

He had noticed the tall, dark man quietly sipping a drink while Belton argued with old Wade Harley and apparently giving the controversy no heed.

"Never dreamed he was the big jigger's sidekick," flashed through Ran's brain as his guns let go with a rippling crash.

The dark man was also shooting with both hands and weaving and ducking. He spun Ran's hat from his head, ripped the sleeve of his shirt and sent a bullet through his loosely swinging vest. Then he went down, blood spouting from his punctured right shoulder. He gamely tried to lift his left gun and Ran shot it from his hand.

Crouched against the wall with his thumbs hooked over the hammers of the big single-actions, Ran surveyed the room. Men were coming out from behind posts and from under tables.

"Anybody else int'rested?" he asked softly.

There was a moment of silence, then a voice answered:

"Not here, but there'll be plenty later. Feller, you'd better ride, and ride fast."

Still sweeping the room with watchful eyes and never for an instant losing sight of the two men on the floor, Ran reloaded.

"Looks like I musta tangled with the big he-wolf of these head diggin's," he murmured. Aloud he said:

"Thanks for the good advice, feller. I ain't takin' it."

"That's talkin', son!" applauded old Wade Harley. "Don'tcha let them damn cow thieves bluff you!"

Bruce Belton sat up, rubbing his sore jaw. Ran

expected curses and was surprised at Belton's wry grin.

"Feller, yore good," said Belton, speaking with difficulty. "I ain't been hit so hard since my mother-in-law come to live with me. I'll know better'n to lead with my jaw next time we tangle."

He got to his feet unsteadily and glanced down at the wounded man, who was sitting up and looking pretty sick.

"Thought I heerd guns goin' off," he rumbled. "What'd you hafta horn in for, Cale?"

The wounded man did not reply. Instead he turned his black eyes on Ran Hollis. Two things impressed Ran at once:

Never in his life had he looked upon a face so startlingly handsome; and never had he beheld such concentrated hate as that which glared at him from those burning eyes.

"Lend a hand, Uncle Bruce," the wounded man said. "I gotta see a doctor."

Belton helped him to his feet and supported him to the door. He nodded at Wade Harley as he passed.

"Better keep yore trap shet next time, Harley," he advised.

"Go to hell!" said old Wade.

Ran grinned at the little cattleman as the swinging doors closed on the pair. Old Wade wiped the blood from his face and grinned back.

"Them horned toads sho' got a bellyful that time," he chuckled. "But what that jigger over by the table said 'bout ridin' ain't lackin' in sense," he added in a graver tone. "They're a bad pair, son, and they got a lot of bad ones to back their play with."

"I sorta figgered that," Ran nodded. "S'posin' you was to give me the lowdown on what it's all about."

"Let's have a drink, fust," said old Wade. "Then, if yore time ain't pertickler occupied, we'll put on the nosebag t'gether and have a little pow-wow."

"You shore get more kick outa a drink when you take her on a plumb empty stomach," Ran remarked.

"Cowpokes is allus hongry," opined old Wade. "And us'ally busted, too," he added with a chuckle. "C'mon, son, I got some *pesos* what ain't spent yet."

They had the drink and adjourned to a nearby restaurant. Over goodly portions of hawg-hip-an'-hen-fruit they talked.

"Who was that long, good-lookin' jigger I hadda perforate?" Ran asked.

"Name's Cale Winters," replied old Wade. "He's Bruce Belton's foreman."

"I heard him call Belton uncle," Ran commented.

"Yeah, he does. I've heerd tell Belton ain't really his uncle. Belton's wife's sister was his mother. Belton sorta raised him, I guess, but there ain't no blood relation 'tween 'em. Belton's a tough jigger and plenty bad, but he's got some good points. Winters is tough and all bad and if he's got any good points, he's shore managed to keep 'em purty successful covered up."

"Looks like a salty *hombre*," Ran agreed.

"Uh-huh, he's that, all right. It's 'bout the only thing passable you can say for him. He's a killer and it don't make no difference to him if yore facin' him or got yore back turned. He ain't afraid to take a chance if yore lookin' his way and he's jest as willin' to throw down on you if yore lookin' the other way. If *you* waren't chain lightnin' on the draw and darn shifty on yore feet, he'da done for you t'day."

"You mean if you hadn't slammed me outa line with his sights when I wasn't lookin' his way you mean," corrected Ran quietly.

"Fergit that," grunted old Wade. "I jest sorta evened up with you. Chances are Belton'd busted me wide open if it hadn't been for you. He's a plumb crazy man when he loses his temper."

"He didn't seem to hold it against me for knockin' him over."

"He wouldn't," Harley agreed instantly. "He ain't the grudge holdin' kind, like Winters, but if you get in his way he'll rub you out like he would a crawl-worm. He won't hold it 'gainst you for bustin' him in the jaw, but he will figger that yore dangerous to buck up against and act accordin'. Yore safe enough from Belton if you don't tangle with him. The jigger you gotta watch out for is Cale Winters. He'll never forget that hole in the shoulder you give him and jest as quick as he's able he'll be lookin' for you, and not with no opry glass, either."

"Callate then you'd advise me to move on?" said Ran, his eyes on his plate.

Old Wade shot him a shrewd glance and a grin twitched the corners of his mouth beneath his grizzled moustache.

"Yeah," he drawled, "I figger that's the best thing you can do."

Ran's eyes came up at that and he saw the old man was laughing at him. He grinned in answer. Harley put a fried egg in his mouth and washed it down with a cup of coffee.

"Speakin' serious," he said, "are you jest passin' through?"

"Depends on whether there's any reason for me stickin' 'round," Ran told him. "I gotta have me a job and have it quick. If I can land one in this section, that's somethin'. If I can't, I'll hafta trail my rope *pronto*, to where I *can* land one."

"They say there's still some purty good claims up in the hills that ain't staked," commented Harley.

Ran shook his head. "I ain't a miner," he said.

"I'm a cowman and I ain't much int'rested in any-thin' else."

Old Wade sighed a sigh of deep relief. "That's the best news I've heerd today," he declared. "Son, I'm sho' needin' riders bad and you'll drop over when you heah the wages I'm willin' to pay. If yore int'rested, I'll start you off as foreman of my spread and you can work up. What you say?"

"I sorta got a notion you've hired you a hand," Ran told him. "Let's ride out and look her over."

Chapter 10

RIDERS OF THE NIGHT

RAN HOLLIS found himself in the rather unique position of foreman of a first-class cow factory with no men to boss. With the exception of the Chinese cook, who talked English that no one, not even himself, could understand, there was nobody on the big spread other than old Wade Harley, the owner. Ran spent two days riding over the range and arrived at a decision.

"We've gotta have men," he told Harley. Old Wade's comments were profane.

"Don't I know it?" he finished up. "But wheah in hell we gonna get them? I've rode my hoss's hoofs off down to the hocks tryin' to locate a puncher what ain't bit by this blankety-blank gold-minin' bug. Theah jest nacherly ain't no sich animile 'round here what ain't already signed up with some other outfit, and even that kind is darn infrequent."

"I'll get them," Ran told him quietly.

"Wheah?" Harley wanted to know.

"From Mexico."

"Mexico!" sputtered old Wade. "You mean greasers? They ain't no good!"

"What you know 'bout Mexicans?" Ran asked him.

"Nothin', 'cept what folks has told me," admitted Harley.

"Don't b'lieve ev'rhthin' you hear," Ran advised him. "I'll get you riders from Mexico that are jest as good as anythin' this side the Line, and jest as trustworthy."

Old Wade argued the matter at first, but finally he gave in.

"All right! All right!" he growled. "Have it yore way. Things can't be any wuss than they are. If you bring up a bunch of bleached Yaquis what run the whole ranch inter *manana* land, anyway you'll keep Bruce Belton's hellions from gettin' it fust, and that'll be somethin'!"

Ran Hollis rode south at dawn the next morning. Inside of thirty-six hours he was back. Soon lithe, dark-faced men began to ride up to the ranchhouse door. They greeted Ran as *"El Capitan,"* and greeted him with deference. Under Ran's rigid supervision they took over the business of the Bar-H with a dispatch and efficiency that evoked grudging admiration from the prejudiced Harley.

"The Mexican *vaquero* is ev'ry bit as good a hand as the American waddie," Ran told him. "All he needs is somebody to hold him in line. That's necessary, 'cause otherwise he's apt to think that fancy ropin' and hell-bent-for-leather ridin' is all that's needed to keep a ranch goin'. Yeah, we'll have a trail herd ready to run inter San Salvador day after t'morrer."

The herd, for which Harley had a waiting market, set out as the sun was splashing the tallest mountain peaks with red-golden dawn flame. Four quiet, efficient young *vaqueros* rode with it.

"Don't waste time, but don't run the fat off them," Ran cautioned, "and don't get so drunk you won't be back here t'morrer night. One night in that hell-hole is enough for you."

"*Si, Capitan,*" they grinned with a flash of white teeth in their dark faces, "we will observe most carefully."

"You'd better," Ran told them grimly.

"*Si, Capitan.*"

Old Wade looked thoughtful as the herd vanished around a bend, a golden dust cloud hanging over it.

"Them fellers shore mind you well," he commented. "Did they work for you below the Line?"

Ran Hollis nodded, his gray eyes suddenly bleak, as with unpleasant memories. The jagged scar on his lean cheek burned red.

"Yeah," he said shortly, "they *worked* for me."

Wade Harley opened his lips to ask another question, and thought better of it. Something told him it would not be answered.

"There's times when that jigger sorta has me buffaloed," he admitted to himself. "Times when he don't seem a young feller a-tall. I got a notion things ain't allus been easy for him. Come to think on it, he ain't never told me anythin' 'bout himself. He jest sprung up that day he knocked Bruce Belton cold there in the saloon. I can't look back a minute farther than that and see him. Well, he shore knows the cow bus'ness, and I guess that's all I got a right to ask. Golly, he's a tall feller! And look at them shoulders—wide as a barn door! Got a nice mouth, too, and mighty fine eyes. Sorta feller gals fall hard for, but I ain't never heerd him say a thing 'bout women. Mebbe he's sensible and lets 'em alone."

Devil's Canyon lies halfway between the Bar-H ranch and San Salvador. It is not a nice place, being a wild jumble of rock fangs and swirling white water. It is salted blue with bones. Sceptics say that the eerie cries floating up from amid the crags and the gnarled growth on moonlit nights are but the squalls of hungry cougars. But there are some who whisper that they are the screams of the ghosts of murdered men who gasped out their lives in Devil's Canyon.

But the ominous gorge provides a short cut which does away with many weary desert miles on the road to San Salvador.

Ran Hollis' *vaqueros* knew this, so they headed

the herd into Devil's Canyon, scornful of ghosts and sinister stories of past happenings.

Midway through the canyon is a weird outcropping of spires and columns known as The Devil's Kitchen.

The trail herd was passing the Kitchen when the canyon suddenly blazed with rifle fire. From behind the dark columns came the spurts of reddish flame and the whorls of blue smoke.

Two of the Mexicans went down before that first storm blast of lead. The others jerked their guns and made a fight of it.

A hopeless fight from the start. They were outnumbered four to one. Their attackers were sheltered. They were in the open. Before their guns were empty, the remaining two *vaqueros* were on the ground.

With wild whoops the masked attackers rode from behind the columns. They sent the herd charging through the canyon and out the far mouth. They did not turn it toward San Salvador.

Pedro Gomez brought the news to the Bar-H. He also brought a smashed shoulder and a furrowed scalp. The raiders had thought him dead. Ran fixed him up temporarily and sent a man on the gallop to San Salvador and a doctor. Then he questioned Pedro who lay smoking a cigarette and making light of his wounds.

"All were masked, *Capitan*," said Pedro. "I saw

no faces. Big men they seemed to be, the most of them. Their hair it was long."

"All Bruce Belton's riders are long-haired hellions," broke in Wade Harley.

"Lots of fellers on this range wear their hair long," Ran reminded him. Pedro was speaking again——

"One, *Capitan*, a tall man, carried his arm in a sling."

"Arm in a sling?"

"*Si*, as if it were broken."

For several minutes Ran Hollis sat silent. Then——

"That's somethin' to go on," he muttered. "Arm in a sling!

"You didn't notice his hair, Pedro, or his eyes?" he asked.

"The eyes, no," replied the *vaquero*. "The hair it was black—most black."

Ran and old Wade exchanged glances. "It shore ties up," said the latter. Ran nodded, a cold glitter birthing in the depths of his steady eyes. He was thoughtful and silent during the late supper. After the meal, while old Wade puttered about in the kitchen with the Chinese cook, he slipped from the house, saddled his golden sorrel and rode away.

Wade Harley had pointed out the route to Belton's Lazy-B ranch several days before and Ran had no trouble following it. Two hours after leaving the Bar-H he pulled up in front of Belton's big white ranchhouse. He dismounted, walked up the veranda steps and through the open front door. He found himself in a wide hall. A short distance down the hall, light poured through a doorway. Ran strode toward the light, puckering his eyes against the glare. He halted in the doorway.

Bruce Belton sat behind a big flat-top desk in the middle of the room. He glared mingled astonishment and anger at the intruder.

"What the hell do *you* want?" he demanded.

Ran eyed him for several moments before speaking. Belton, hard as he was, moved uncomfortably under that chill gaze. Ran's voice was deceptively soft:

"Cale Winters' shoulder ain't healin' so fast, is it, Belton? Been better'n a month now since I drilled him and he's still carryin' his arm in a sling."

"What the hell of it?" growled Belton. "You come bustin' in on me this way jest to tell me somethin' I already know?"

"Nope," Ran replied. "I come to find out somethin' I didn't know for shore. I wanted to learn if Winters really was carryin' his arm in a sling."

Belton stared in amazement. "What good does it do you now you know it?"

"Jest this, Belton," Ran went on in the same soft drawl, "a tall, black-haired jigger with his arm in a sling helped to rustle a herd of Bar-H cattle in

Devil's Canyon t'day. And inc'dentally," he added, his voice losing something of the softness, "three of my riders got killed durin' the arg'ment."

"Huh," grunted Belton, "I hear tell as how yore ridin' Mexicans on yore range. What's a few greasers more or less matter?"

Ran Hollis' cold eyes suddenly blazed. He took a step forward, shaking with a rage that sent Belton cowering back in his chair. One of his long-barreled black Colts slid from its sheath. The single-action clicked back to full cock.

"Belton," he whispered, his voice the grind of knife-edged steel on ice, "I got a notion to gun-shoot you wheah you set and leave you to die sweatin'! You yaller hyderphobia skunk, I——"

The big Colt jutted forward. Its black muzzle yawned at Belton.

Crash!

Ran reeled back, blood welling from a bullet-burned crease above his left temple. He flung his gun away from Belton to cover a smoke-misted form framed in an inner doorway. His finger curled on the trigger. Then with unbelievable speed he wrenched the gun muzzle sideways as it spouted flame.

There was a cry from the doorway and the figure crouching there crumpled up in a pathetic little heap. The lamplight glowed on a white face framed in darkly red curls.

Bellowing with anguish, Bruce Belton leaped to his feet and dashed across the room. Quick as he was, Ran Hollis was ahead of him. The cowboy raised the slight figure of the red-haired girl in his arms, his eyes and his slim, sinewy fingers searching frantically for the wound.

"Is she dead?" bawled Belton. "Damn you, did you kill her?"

"I didn't even hit her!" Ran flung at him over his shoulder. "There ain't a scratch on her anywhere. She—hold on, here's a bruised place on her forehead!"

"That ain't no bullet wound," declared Belton, stooping, "mebbe she hit her head when she fell."

"Didn't fall on her head," Ran grunted. His eyes swept the floor nearby and centered on a big blue gun with a smashed lock. He laughed with utter relief.

"Look there," he told Belton, pointing. "That's the gun she used. My bullet knocked it outa her hand. It hit the door jamb and bounced back and slammed her 'side the head. Look, she's comin' outa it!"

The girl's amazingly long black lashes were fluttering against her creamily tanned cheeks. They opened wide and two big blue eyes stared up into Ran's blood-streaked face. Ran recognized the girl who had rescued him from the Mexican *rurales*.

"Oh!" she gasped. "I—I didn't kill you!"

"Not hardly, Ma'am," Ran told her gravely, "but you come closet."

The girl shuddered. Then anger glowed in the blue eyes.

"I ought to have," she declared. "You were going to shoot Uncle Bruce."

"Good Lord!" muttered Ran under his breath. "He's *her* uncle, too! Then that sidewinder Winters must be her—hell, it jest can't be!"

He picked her up, carried her to a nearby couch and laid her upon it. She was tiny and slender but with plenty of curves where curves were in order. Ran decided during those few brief seconds that she was a perfect fit in his arms.

"You feelin' better now, Ma'am?" he asked.

"I'm all right," she said, sitting up. "What are you doing here?"

Ran did not answer. Bruce Belton's voice filled the pause.

"Feller," he suggested, "seems to me you've raised enough hell 'round here for one evenin'. Wouldn't be a half bad idear if you forked yore bronk and sidled off. Ray," he addressed the girl, "I figger you'd better hightail up to yore room and put a wet towel on yore head. Get goin', now."

"What about leaving you here alone with this man?" she objected.

"Don'tcha worry 'bout this man," Belton told

her. "Him and me ain't gonna have no more trouble t'night. You done busted that all up."

The girl swung her slim little feet to the floor and stood up. The top of her bright head came barely to Ran's shoulder. From somewhere she produced a tiny white handkerchief. With deft fingers she removed the scarf from about her throat and before he realized what she was up to, she had placed the folded handkerchief over the slight crease her bullet had made and bound it in place with the scarf.

"That'll keep it from bleeding," she said, and was gone, casting a fleeting glance over her shoulder as she vanished through the inner door. Ran stood staring after her, a dazed expression on his face.

Bruce Belton's face was a study. Twice he opened his mouth to speak and twice he closed it again. Wordless, he watched Ran Hollis walk from the room. Still wordless, he listened to the click of departing hoofs. He started as a silvery voice spoke behind him:

"Isn't he just the best-looking thing that ever lived, Uncle Bruce!"

Chapter 11

ON THE TRAIL

RAN HOLLIS rode away from the Lazy-B ranch in a mental turmoil. He had gone there to find out if Cale Winters and his men really were the wide-loopers who had murdered his men, and with the intention of executing summary vengeance on Winters, Belton, and all concerned. He had attained the first objective and signally failed in the second.

"It was that gang, all right," he muttered. "Theah wasn't a soul on the place 'sides Belton and the girl. If there'd been anybody in the bunkhouse all that gunplay woulda brought 'em hootin'. The outfit jest nacherly hadn't got back from their little job, that's what. I'd oughta blowed Belton out from under his hat, but hell, I couldn't do it with *her* there!

"She darned near blowed me out from under mine," he added with a reminiscent chuckle. He shuddered as he thought of the horrible thing his own bullet came so near to doing. Then he sighed deeply.

"If this ain't a mess!" he growled. "Winters

must be her brother if Belton is uncle to 'em both. What the hell *am* I gonna do 'bout it? Man, but she's one sweet armful!"

Then he resolutely dismissed the red-haired girl from his thoughts and set his mind on the problem at hand. He pushed the big sorrel and it was but little after midnight when he reached the Bar-H ranchhouse.

Pedro was resting easy.

"Doc says he'll pull through all right," Wade Harley told him. "All he needs is rest and a little watchin' over. Hell Hang High, the cook, is a fust class nurse and he'll look after him."

"Me velly good," nodded the Chinaman. "Me damn velly good. Me no thlow lolling stone at glass house outa fire into flying pan, me betcha me you!"

"It don't sound so damn good," sighed Ran, "but I guess it's all right."

"He read that somewhere—Shakespeare or the Bible or somethin'," explained old Wade.

Ran went to the bunkhouse and routed out Angel. Angel, an almost full-blood Yaqui Indian, had no other name that anybody had even been able to learn, and he made no particular effort to live up to the one he did possess—his wings hadn't sprouted yet! But he was one of the best trackers in all Mexico and about all he knew of fear was what he had heard somebody say about it.

There was a brief exchange of words and then the tall American and the stocky Mexican saddled up fresh horses and rode for Devil's Canyon.

They reached the gloomy gorge at daybreak. The desert was glorious as a bridegroom in vestments of scarlet and gold as they rode through the far mouth and into the full blaze of the newly risen sun.

"It's so darn purty it hurts," murmured Ran Hollis.

"*Si*," agreed Angel, "lovely as the eyes of a *senorita* when the guitars sing softly and the *mescal* sparkles golden in the glass. Do you remember, *Capitan*——"

"Nev' mind! nev' mind!" Ran interrupted hastily. "You start on that line and we won't get nowhere. What you make of these tracks?"

"The task it is simple," scoffed Angel. "Verily a child could follow so plain a trail. It reminds me of the old days, *Capitan*, but then we stalked a nobler quarry than a mere herd of *ganado*. It was gun and knife at the end then, *Capitan*, and the shake of Death's bony hand for the loser! *Ai!* those were the days!"

Here where the desert ran along the foot of the hills, the soil was stony and iron hard, but Angel followed the trail with little difficulty.

"They go far, *Capitan*," he told Ran. "See, they

slowed the herd, which shows that they did not expect to soon reach their destination."

"They hadn't got back to the Lazy-B yet when I rode up there, seven or eight hours after the raid," Ran agreed. "Wish they'd have headed toward Mexico instead of goin' nawth."

Angel grinned wolfishly. "*Si,* then we would have brought the brethren down upon them, and——"

He drew his hand across his throat in an expressive gesture.

Chapter 12
LEAPING FLAME

THE sun climbed the long ladder of the sky, paused blisteringly to catch his breath and shambled down-hill toward the west. Ran and Angel, weary, hungry, red-eyed from lack of sleep, still followed the dim trail. As the purple shadows began to crawl up the western slopes they came opposite a dark canyon mouth.

"It goes into the *barranca*," nodded Angel. "From now, *Capitan*, we must proceed with care."

"Yeah, we're liable to get ourselves drygulched if we don't," Ran agreed.

Between the towering rock walls of the canyon they rode, peering, listening, alert for sight or sound of danger; but only the grumble of water torturing over the stones and the rustle of the wind reached their ears. Those and the hollow echoes their passing flung back from the beetling cliffs.

The sun sank behind the mountain wall and shadows poured into the gorge.

"We'll be goin' it blind in another half hour," Ran muttered.

"If we can not see, neither can others," Angel remarked.

"Yeah," Ran admitted, "but they can hear."

"I hear even now!" exclaimed Angel.

From afar off drifted a thin wailing sound. Ran listened intently, heard it repeated and recognized it as the tired bawl of distant cattle.

"We're catchin' up with them!" he exulted.

"They have made camp," Angel said. "The sounds do not move on."

A little later they sniffed the fragrant tang of wood smoke. Added to it was a tantalizing aroma of frying meat and boiling coffee.

"I'm so hongry my stomach figgers I done got my throat cut," sighed Ran.

"Me I am empty like the log that is hollow," said Angel.

The canyon began to narrow. Soon it was less than two-score yards from wall to wall. The growth thinned.

"*Capitan*, we had best leave the horses here in this thicket," said Angel.

They did so and proceeded on foot. Ten minutes later a point of light winked at them through the low growth. It grew larger as they approached and resolved into a camp fire around which dark figures moved.

"Seven of 'em," Ran counted. "Feller we done bit off more'n we can chaw."

"So it would seem," agreed Angel, "but in the old days *El Cascabel* reckoned not with odds. His cunning made of them nothing. Nor has that cunning deserted him here in this colder land, I am sure."

"Thanks for the good opinion," Ran grunted, "but darned if this ain't got me stumped so far. Two 'gainst seven ain't so good. Look, they're sendin' out a night herd. Them jiggers know their bus'ness and ain't takin' no chances. C'mon, feller, let's foller him and see where the dogies are."

They found the herd a few hundred yards up the canyon from the rustlers' camp. It was feeding on a heavy growth of dry grass that rippled ghostily in the faint breeze that blew down the gorge.

"*Capitan,*" whispered Angel, "here are many more *ganado* than we lost. These *ladrones* have doubtless raided into *Mejico.*"

"Uh-huh," Ran whispered back, "unbranded stuff nobody can claim. Well, we'll jest take them along as int'rest."

"But how, *Capitan?*"

For several minutes Ran lay staring at the quiet cattle and the slowly riding night herd. He fingered the tall grass stems which provided them concealment.

"Angel," he whispered, "this stuff is dry as powder and the canyon's damn narrow. The wind blows *down* the canyon, too, towards them hellions' camp."

Angel hissed in his breath like a snake. "You mean, *Capitan*——"

"Uh-huh," Ran nodded, "jest that. It won't be givin' 'em much chance, but——"

"They gave our brothers no chance at all there in Devil's Canyon," interrupted Angel.

Ran nodded, his lean face bleak.

"Hafta wait," he decided. "Long towards mawnin', when it's darkest and ev'body's sleepin' sound, that's the best time. What'll we do till then?"

"Sleep," replied Angel instantly, "farther up the *barranca* under the bushes. I will awaken when the smell of dawn is in the air."

"You'd better," Ran cautioned, "or the next thing you smell is liable to be brimstone."

It seemed to Ran that he had hardly closed his eyes when he felt Angel's touch on his shoulder.

"It is time, *Capitan*," breathed the Mexican.

Ran sat up, rubbing his eyes. It was still pitch dark but there was a freshness in the air that said morning was not far off. The sky was overcast but there was no rain.

"C'mon," he told Angel, "fust thing is that darn night herd. We can't leave him to yell and rouse the others up too quick."

Silently as snakes, they crept through the tall grass until they were but a few yards distant from the bunched cattle. Ran had hoped that the guard might be asleep; but he still rode slowly, slumped in his saddle, weary but alert. Ran wracked his brain for a plan to remove that menace. The guard was riding toward them and a little to one side. Ran plotted his course and with a whispered warning to Angel glided off through the grass. He reached the shadow of a small tree and swarmed up the trunk. Balancing on a low branch he waited.

On came the night herd. Ran thrilled exultantly when he saw for sure that he had calculated rightly: the guard would pass under the tree!

On came the clumping hoofs. The horseman bent his head to avoid a sagging branch, and two sets of steely fingers wound about his throat, stifling the yell that rose to his startled lips. Ran Hollis flung his sinewy body down and sideways, wrenching with all his strength.

There was a crunching *plop* the instant before they hit the ground together. The frightened horse snorted away a few paces and pricked his ears toward the flopping patter of boot heels beating on the soft ground. The flopping ceased and Ran rose to his feet. The night herd lay still, his head lolling hideously on his broken neck.

"Waren't no other way to do it," Ran muttered, wiping the moisture from his forehead. "One yell outa him and the game'd been up."

He caught the horse and led it back up the canyon. "No sense in you gettin' scorched, feller," he told it. Then he rejoined Angel.

Working swiftly and silently, they gathered bunches of the dry grass. A match flickered and another. The bunches of grass flared high. Then a thin line of flame ran from wall to wall of the canyon. The wind caught it, fanned it, sent it snapping and crackling down the canyon toward the cattle. Frightened bawls arose, a wild milling. Then the herd turned tail and ran from the approaching terror. The mighty thunder of the stampeding hoofs roared between the rock walls.

Straight for the rustlers' camp rolled the bellowing, charging mass. Slashing hoofs and tossing horns! Wild red eyes and flaring nostrils! It was a vision straight from hell for the doomed men hurled headlong from their peaceful sleep.

Above the bawling thunder rose frantic yells that soared to shrieks of agony snuffed out with appalling suddenness. The herd swept on toward the distant mouth of the canyon. The fire poured over the camp and died wispily amid the greener growth farther down the gorge.

Ran and Angel stamped out the flames that burned but feebly against the wind. Then they picked their way through the smoldering embers toward what remained of the camp.

Light was pouring from the brightening sky like silvery water into the gorge. Under its soft glow the camp was a scene of blasted horror. Ran turned aside, more than a little sick, but Angel stared at the scorched and trampled bodies with grim satisfaction.

"Our brothers are avenged, *Capitan*," he said. "It is the justice of *El Cascabel*."

" 'The Rattlesnake' rides not in this land," Ran reminded him quietly. "You forget."

"*Si*," replied Angel. "I dream of another day and another land. Now, *Capitan*, let us go and gather together our *ganado*."

"Yeah," Ran approved, "the dogies are next in order. And we'll jest run the whole lot of 'em inter San Salvador and turn 'em over to Brewster. He'll have 'em chopped up inter beefsteaks 'fore this time t'morrer."

The cattle had run away from their fright before they reached the mouth of the canyon and were found quietly grazing on the rich bunch grass. Ran and Angel rounded them up and headed them across the desert toward San Salvador.

Chapter 13

THE PLOT

CALE WINTERS, his arm still strapped across his breast, sat in a San Salvador saloon and stared at a grimy poster he held in his left hand.

"Wheah'd you say you got it, Connors?" he asked of the hard-eyed, long-haired man who sat across the table from him.

"Jest t'other side the Mexican border. Lots of 'em tacked up on trees down theah. The Diaz gov'ment sho' wants that jigger bad. No wonder, though. He musta give them crooked *alcaldes* and *jefe politicos* and sich the creeps. Seems ev'ry time he'd heah of one of them mayors or police chiefs pullin' somethin' shady on the *peons*—and they pull plenty down there—him and his hellions would come larrupin' down on top of 'em, clean out their garrison and hang the crooks. The *peons* think *El Cascabel* is jest about God A'mighty on earth, but the gov'ment officials figger him for the Devil. I heard Mexico City has sent so many *rurales* to look for him that he busted up his outfit and trailed his rope.

129

After all, guess he figgered he couldn't fight the whole Mexican army."

Winters translated into English the Spanish words printed on the poster:

REWARD
DEAD OR ALIVE
5,000 *Pesos*
for
EL CASCABEL (THE RATTLESNAKE)

Followed a description of the wanted "bandit" and his "crimes." Above the heavy block lettering was portrayed a lean, bronzed face out of which gazed level gray eyes. The rather wide mouth was thin-lipped and firm, the jaw tight.

"You think it's him?" asked Connors.

Cale Winters swore viciously. "Of co'hse it's him! You think I'll ever forgit them cat eyes of his? You have 'em look at you 'crost a gun sight and you won't forgit 'em either! See that scar on his cheek, too!"

"What we gonna do 'bout it?" wondered Connors. "Five thousand *pesos* is a plumb heap of money."

"I'd give that much and more to see him squirm on the hot end of a bullet," declared Winters. "He went up to the ranchhouse last night and had a row with Uncle Bruce."

"The hell he did! What'd the Old Man do 'bout it?"

"Damned if I've been able to get the straight of *what* happened," admitted Winters. "Uncle Bruce jest grunts. Seems Ray was mixed up in it somehow. She's been moonin' 'round like a sick calf ev'ry since. She's got a bruise 'side her haid and theah's a bullet hole in the wall in the front room. When I asked her what the hell went on, she snapped somethin' at me and flounced off upstairs.

"She won't get by with that kinda stuff oncet we're married," he rasped between his teeth, his handsome face drenched by the ugliness of passion.

" 'Bout this heah *El Cascabel*," reminded Connors.

"Let's go see the sheriff," suggested Winters. "He's a purty good friend of mine. C'mon, Uncle Bruce and Ray are ridin' to town this evenin' and I'm s'posed to meet them."

They left the saloon and walked down a side street toward the sheriff's office. Winters shaded his hand and peered at an approaching dust cloud.

"There comes the boys with the herd," he remarked. "Wait a minute, let's amble down and see 'em run inter Brewster's corral 'fore we go to the sheriff."

The cattle reached the big corral before they did. Connors suddenly swore a bewildered oath.

"Cale, them ain't our boys with 'em!" he ex-

ploded. "It's a Mexican and—and—by Gawd! it's
him!"

They stared in utter amazement at the cattle
streaming through the corral gate and the two dusty
riders urging them along.

"W-what yuh s'pose happened?" stuttered Connors at last.

Cale Winters' was black with rage. He spun on
his heel and strode back up the street.

"C'mon," he flung at Connors. "Don't let 'em
see us standin' here lookin'. Let's hunt up the
sheriff."

Chapter 14

TRAPPED

TOM BREWSTER, who did the wholesale butchering for San Salvador, welcomed Ran enthusiastically.

"Man, I'm glad you got in with this lot!" he exclaimed. "We're shore needin' this meat bad!"

"Hello!" he said a few minutes later. "This tally is jest 'bout twict what Harley said he'd send. How come?"

"Can't you handle this many?" Ran asked.

"Hell, yes!" Brewster assured him, "and more, too. I'm almighty glad to get 'em. Cale Winters promised to have a herd in t'day, too, but so far it ain't showed up."

"Mebbe somethin' delayed him," Ran remarked dryly.

Hoofs sounded in the street outside Brewster's little office. Ran glanced through the window and caught a flash of red hair framing an elfish little face.

"There goes Bruce Belton and his niece, Ray Car-

133

rol," said Brewster. "They say she's gonna marry Cale Winters."

Ran stood up. "Think I'll sorta look the *pueblo* over t'night," he remarked casually. Angel grinned his delight.

"Things oughta be lively," Brewster called after them as they passed through the door. "T'day's payday for the mines."

Things *were* lively, and they quickly proceeded to get livelier. As the blue dust of the dusk sifted down from the mountain tops, the narrow streets became crowded. Miners whose pockets were filled with gold that itched to be spent jostled one another. Lights blazed in saloon and dancehall and gambling hell. Song blared through the open doors. The strum of guitars and the shriller tones of violins joined with the pert notes of the banjo. Boots thumped and high heels clicked.

"Let 'er rip!" bawled a drunken miner, elbowing his way to a bar. "She comes easy and she goes easy! Belly up, gents, I'm buyin'!"

Whiskey flowed like water. Gold flowed even faster across the bars, onto the gambling tables, into the hands of the dancehall girls. Nobody knew how much he spent and nobody gave a damn! There was plenty more gold in the hills. Why worry about what one carried in his pockets! Let 'er rip! San Salvador boiled and bubbled in the grim shadow of the mighty mountains, the blare of her lights beating

back the glow of the frightened stars. At her feet
stretched the shimmering glory of the moon
drenched desert, but San Salvador was too busy
raisin' hell and puttin' a chunk under a corner to give
heed to the feast of beauty spread before her eyes.

Striving hard to convince himself that he was
having a good time, Ran Hollis strolled from saloon
to saloon, drinking morosely, gambling without interest and dancing automatically with the girls who
approached him. Angel had long since been carried
off by a sloe-eyed little *senorita* and he was alone.
Tall, lithe, panther-graceful, he caused more than
one pair of eyes to grow brighter and a trifle wistful
as he sauntered past. Men commented on his
height, breadth of shoulder and the heavy guns that
snugged so closely against his muscular thighs.

"Wade Harley's new foreman, the feller what
licked Bruce Belton and Gale Winters," the whisper
went around. "Wouldn't wanta have them two jiggers on *my* trail!"

Unnoticed by Ran, a man followed him from
place to place. It was Connors, the long-haired
Lazy-B gunman. Cale Winters was still waiting for
the sheriff, who was out of town.

The sheriff rode in about midnight and listened
rather dubiously to Winters' story. He was none
too honest and rather stupid.

"Nope, we don't want no *El Cascabels* hangin'
'round heah," he admitted, "and five thousand *pesos*

is quite a heap of money, but how we gonna cash in on it?"

"You arrest the jigger and lock him up and I'll take care of the rest," Cale assured him. "You jest leave the collectin' to me. Yeah, it's fifty-fifty between us. I'll tell yore dep'ty to come along."

Ran entered the Coronado dancehall and saloon around midnight. It was the show place of San Salvador and "catered to ladies." A number, the wives and daughters of mine owners and business men of the town, were there. Mostly they sat at the tables and looked on, but there were some who danced. The place was plentifully supplied with "girls," too, whose business it was to dance with unattached males, of whom there were many. They were a carefree lot who chose to forget the past, live for the present and not worry about the future. For the first time that night, Ran Hollis began to really enjoy himself somewhat. Then he glanced toward one of the tables and the lights went out again!

Seated at that table was Ray Carrol, her curly hair gleaming like burnished copper, her blue eyes glowing. She was talking animatedly with a good looking young cowboy with rather long hair.

Ran elbowed his way to the bar and glowered into his drink. He turned at a light touch on his arm.

A laughing-eyed little Mexican girl stood at his elbow.

"You dance weeth me, tall *senor, si?*" she invited.

"Shore," Ran told her, "why not?"

The orchestra broke into a waltz. Ran slipped a long arm around the girl's slim waist and they glided out onto the floor. Intent on his partner for the moment, he did not see Ray Carrol's white little teeth suddenly grip her red under lip. When he did glance in her direction she was laughing merrily at something the cowboy was saying.

Ran Hollis danced with the same panther-grace with which he walked, and in the little *senorita* he had found a fitting partner. Soon the other couples were edging away from the pair, giving them room, watching them with admiration. The girl noted it and threw her very soul into the dance. Her little feet seemed to skim the floor as if it were cushioned with air, her big eyes glowed, her high, round little breasts arched as she flung back her dark head and swayed against Ran's muscular arm. A ripple of applause ran around the room. Ran's arm tightened, drawing her closer; and any woman would have had little trouble interpreting the look on Ray Carrol's face at that moment!

Suddenly with a shimmering flash of burnished hair, there was another dancer on the floor. Ray Carrol danced solo and she danced as must dance the Queen of Fay in her green ballroom on nights of fretted moonfire with frogs a-drum and elf horns blowing. She was a flame, a bright sunbeam, the dawn wind walking silver-shod amid the flowers.

The musicians quickened their tempo. A Mexican with a voice like a laughing wind in the rain-washed sky began to sing:

"Oh, love that steps from star to star
    And walks where the dew-kissed roses are——"

The red-haired girl seemed to flit from word to word and swing in the arms of song. She whirled on slim little feet, her short skirt billowing out from slender ankles and silken legs, her glowing curls wantoning over her white forehead. Her red lips were slightly parted, her wide eyes burning blue as a stainless star.

"She ees wonderful!" breathed the little *senorita*. Then with sudden understanding:

"*Senor*, she ees dancing for *you!*"

"Yore dreamin', honey," Ran scoffed.

The little Mexican laughed a trill of impish laughter. Suddenly she swung him about with supple strength and slipped from his arms as Ray Carrol whirled past. The next instant Ran's eyes were full of flying red curls and his arms full of slim, vibrant girl. They swung into step instinctively.

"Well, I think it was about time!" said Ray.

To the crowd the whole thing looked like a pre-arranged play. A roar of applause burst forth.

Men whooped and slapped their thighs. Women clapped their hands.

As the applause died down a harsh voice sounded: "Sorta hate to bust up the show!"

A hand fell on Ran's shoulder. He turned and a gun barrel prodded him in the belly. Before him stood a big beefy man with a star pinned to his vest.

"Jest keep yore hands up wheah they are," said the sheriff. "Raise the right one a little higher. Sorry, Miss," he apologized to Ray, "but law bus'ness is law bus'ness."

Ray's indignant voice broke in before Ran could speak.

"What's the meaning of this?" she demanded. "What has he done?"

"Ma'am, you any idea who you been dancin' with?" the sheriff asked. Without waiting for a reply he answered the question:

"Ma'am, you been dancin' with *El Cascabel!*"

"*El Cascabel!*" Ray whispered the words through stiff lips, her face paper-white. "*El Cascabel*, the Mexican bandit!"

"Uh-huh," nodded the sheriff, "with five thousand *pesos* reward on his haid. The Mexican gov'ment wants him for a few little murders and robberies and sich."

"Sheriff, yore talkin' through yore hat and you know it," Ran broke in. "Ev'body on the border knows what I did in Mexico and there ain't a co'ht in Arizona what would turn me over to Diaz and his hellions."

"We'll see 'bout that," said the sheriff. "Get his guns, Hank."

The deputy, a lantern-jawed individual whose heart didn't seem in the business, reluctantly removed Ran's guns from their sheaths.

"Damnhoolishness!" the cowboy heard him mutter under his breath.

Ray Carrol spoke up.

"Isn't—isn't there something I can do?"

"Theah ain't nothin' to worry 'bout," Ran assured her. "It'll all be ironed out in a jiffy. Shore sorry this hadda happen right now, though."

"Get goin'," said the sheriff.

Standing well back in the shadows across the street, Cale Winters grinned wolfishly as he saw the sheriff heading his prisoner for the jail. He turned and hurried away.

Chapter 15

THE RESCUE

THE sheriff hung Ran's gun belt over his desk and locked him in the iron cage which formed the inner room of the little calaboose. Ran sat down on the hard bunk and rolled a cigarette.

"All right, Hank, you can get back to yore poker game," the sheriff told the deputy.

The deputy left. The sheriff puttered around a bit and then lay down on a cot. Soon he was snoring. Ran tried the door and window of the cage, found them decidedly solid, and curled up on his own bunk.

He did not go to sleep directly. Ray Carrol's white face and great, startled eyes haunted him. He knew that the stories that circled about the head of *El Cascabel* were not all nice stories. When a man rides through years of blood and powder smoke, no matter how just may be the cause in which he rides, it cannot be otherwise. The vicious, the intolerant, the despotic below the Line hated the very name of "The Rattlesnake" with a hate that was venomous in its intensity. To them he was a

141

fiend incarnate, a red-handed killer, a rebel against accepted authority as personified in themselves and their own callous selfishness. They did not speak kindly of him.

"Hard to tell what all she's heard and b'lieves," Ran mused. "Well, theah ain't no help for it. I wonder who's back of this bus'ness? I sho' don't give that dumb sheriff credit for that much brains. Mebbe he's jest dumb enough to really think he's doin' his duty, though. Oh, to hell with it all!"

Ran rolled over and went to sleep. He was thoroughly worn out after the excitement of the past two days and nights and he slept soundly.

Nevertheless, the sound of voices in the outer room awakened him. He sat up, slipped on his boots and walked to the grated door. A light burned dimly in the outer room and he could see two shadowy figures.

One was the sheriff, who appeared very angry and more than a little frightened. He was sitting stupidly on the edge of his bunk and yammering at the other occupant of the room, who was swathed in a long black cloak, wore a wide-brimmed hat pulled low over the eyes and a handkerchief swathing the lower half of the face. A gloved hand held a big blue gun that menaced the sheriff.

"Get goin'," said a voice muffled in the folds of the handkerchief. "Open that door and be quick about it."

"You'll be sorry for this, feller," sputtered the sheriff, creaking to his feet. "You'll be——"

"You'll be still sorrier if you don't get a move on," broke in the other. "I got a itchy trigger finger."

Ran heard the ominous double click as the big single-action went to full cock. The sheriff heard it, too. He shuffled across the floor on bare feet, a bunch of keys jingling in his hand. He fumbled at the cage door for a moment, a bolt clicked and the door swung back.

"Come out," the voice of the masked gun wielder ordered. Ran instinctively obeyed.

The other plucked the sheriff's Colt from its sheath, shoved him into the cage and slammed the door.

"You can't do this!" yammered the sheriff. "I tell you——"

"I'm tellin' you—to keep quiet," his captor interrupted.

"Say, there really ain't no sense in all this," Ran protested. "No co'ht would——"

"No court will have a chance to, if you stay here," interrupted the other. "That reward notice says *'dead or alive!'* There's a mob headed this way right now to take you out of here and turn you over to the Mexican authorities—*dead!* That fat fool in there wouldn't protect you from them. I've half a notion he's in on the deal. Hurry, there is no time to lose!"

Ran hesitated no longer. He jerked his gun belt from the peg over the desk and buckled it on.

"Be seein' you, sheriff," he called as they passed through the outer door.

The sheriff's reply did not bear repeating.

Horses were pawing at the hitch-rack in front of the jail. Ran and his masked rescuer mounted quickly.

"Listen!" exclaimed the other.

The air was a-drum with the low thunder of swift hoofs. Even as they hesitated, a dark body of horsemen swept around a corner and bore down on the jail.

"Ride!" barked Ran. "It's them!"

They rode, bending low over their horses' necks. A yell went up as they swept through a pool of light cast by a rickety street lamp. Guns roared. Bullets screamed past.

They took a skittering corner at a mad gallop. The bullets stopped for a moment, then started again as the pursuers stormed after them.

Ran heard a sudden smacking thud as a bullet went home. Down went his companion's horse in a wallowing heap. The rider was hurled headlong but fortunately landed on hands and knees, rolled over and staggered erect. Ran jerked his own pony to a foaming, skating halt, leaned far over, wrapped a long arm about the other's waist and heaved with all his strength.

Up came the slim figure, like a wind-blown feather. Unprepared for so light a weight, Ran was almost unhorsed. He regained his balance with a wrenching twist and drove his spurs home. The outraged pony snorted his anger and shot forward. Ran jerked a gun, writhed around in the saddle and sent a stream of lead into the ranks of the pursuers, who were almost within arm's reach.

Down went a horse. Another stumbled over it. For a moment wild confusion reigned. Yells of rage and pain boiled up. Guns banged. Horses squealed.

The fugitives gained precious yards while the pursuers were untangling themselves. Ran had time to glance down at the form he gripped so tightly against his breast.

"Well for the love of Pete!" he gasped.

The wide hat had fallen off and the first pale light of dawn smoldered on a mass of tumbled red curls. He ripped the masking handkerchief away and Ray Carrol's wide blue eyes looked into his.

Ran's arm tightened still more and regardless of the yelling pursuit, the bullets that were again whipping past and the bridle-swinging, galloping horse, he leaned over and placed a very lingering and very loving kiss squarely on her red mouth. He got the kiss back, with interest!

The horse stumbled and Ran snatched at the dangling bridle. He steadied the bronk and cast a glance over his shoulder. The pursuit had straightened out again and was gaining.

"Hoss carryin' too much load," he muttered. "They'll be right on top of us in a jiffy at this rate!"

A few miles ahead loomed a black jumble of hills slashed with canyons and *barrancas*. Once there, they might find safety in some gorge.

"We ain't never gonna make it in time, though," the cowboy admitted to himself.

Ray was struggling in his arms.

"Put me down," she urged. "They won't hurt me and you'll have a chance if the horse isn't carrying double."

"You shet up!" growled Ran. "Want me to start spankin' you 'fore I've got the right to?"

Ray blushed, but did not seem displeased. Ran cast another anxious glance over his shoulder. Then he faced resolutely to the front.

The hills were nearer now, but the pursuit was still nearer. Bullets were coming alarmingly close. Ran shuddered at what a lucky chance shot might do. He glanced about in the strengthening light. Suddenly he jerked the horse sharply to the side.

Not three hundred yards distant ran Devil's Creek in its deep gorge. Fully fifty feet high were the straight-up-and-down rock walls of the narrow canyon the rushing water had cut in the desert floor.

At the bottom of the gorge the stream flowed swift and deep. Not until it reached the fanged and spired jumble of the hills did the gorge widen to form the true Devil's Canyon.

"Hold on tight!" Ran barked and headed the racing horse straight for the yawning chasm.

The bronk did not want to take the leap, but under the lash of quirt and spur he took it. Ray cried out and clung convulsively to Ran as they shot over the lip.

Down! down! the air screaming in their ears, the dark water rushing up to meet them. They struck with a prodigious splash and vanished. Yells and curses sounded as the astounded pursuers frantically pulled their ponies to a halt on the very lip of the gorge.

The horse came up, blowing and snorting. He plunged wildly and went under again. He came up half drowned. Ran slipped from his back and rested one hand on the saddle, gripping Ray tightly with the other.

Relieved of their weight, the horse steadied and began to swim. The current gripped all three and whirled them down stream.

On the lip of the gorge, Cale Winters cursed like a madman.

"Who in hell was that jigger what turned him loose?" he demanded of all and sundry.

"Hard to tell," said one of his long-haired riders.

"One of them greasers what rides for him, chances are. Where you made yore mistake, Cale, was in not settin' somebody 'sides that fat sheriff to watch the jail."

"I had a feller keepin' a eye on that Mex. that rode inter town with him," raved Winters. "All the rest of his men were at the Bar-H."

"You nev' can tell who's in cahoots with a feller like that," remarked the other wisely. "Chances are you'll be almighty s'prised when you larn who really turned him loose."

Cale was due to be more than surprised!

As the swift current swept them down stream, Ran began to wonder if he hadn't jumped out of Hell Hang High's "flying pan" into a very wet "flire." The water was turbulent and icy. The sheer walls stretched on into the distance without a break. His strength was ebbing.

Ray's face was blue with cold, her lips gray. He could hear her teeth clicking together; but she smiled a brave if wan smile and gamely helped him fight the current.

The horse began to go under. Plainly he was just about at the end of his rope. Ran had to veer away to escape the slashing hoofs. Without the support of the saddle under his hand, the task of keeping their heads above the surface was increasingly difficult. Suddenly they went under. They came up gasping, and almost immediately went under again. Ran fought with all his waning strength to struggle up again, and at that instant his feet touched bottom.

Panting, staggering, clinging to the almost unconscious girl, he sloshed through the shallowing water and sank utterly exhausted on a narrow strip of sand that skirted the canyon wall.

For a long time he lay there, the girl snugged in his arms. Her eyes were closed, but she breathed steadily and a tinge of color glowed in her cheeks. Her lips were growing rose-red once more. She sighed and the big blue eyes fluttered open. One slim little hand reached up to caress his wet black hair.

They found the horse a little farther down stream, nosing at some tufts of discouraged looking grass. He greeted them with a disgusted snort.

"Don't blame you, feller," chuckled Ran. "Guess you figger you'd better sprout wings 'fore you go ridin' with us again."

Ran asked Ray a question as they rode through the canyon, the hot sun drying their clothes:

"How'd you know what was gonna happen?"

"I saw Cale Winters and Bert Connors following you and the sheriff up the street," she told him. "They talked together a while and then Connors rode away. I knew Cale hated you and was up to something. I followed Connors to the ranch. When the boys saddled up and rode away with him toward town, I knew what they were going to do. I got an old cloak, and a hat that would cover my eyes, and cut around ahead of them. I knew I had to beat them into town. I did, but with not much to spare."

They were near the mouth of the canyon when Ran asked another question:

"I heah tell yore gonna marry Cale Winters— are you?"

"I used to think I was," Ray admitted. "It was sort of arranged years ago, when we were both very young. Uncle Bruce wanted it. I changed my mind a little while ago."

Ran debated that for a few minutes. "When'd you change yore mind?" he asked at length.

Color flamed in Ray's soft cheeks. She did not answer at once. When she did her voice was low, and vibrant with an exquisite note that had in it something of both laughter and tears.

"I—I think it was night before last," she said.

They were just leaving the canyon. Glancing up they saw men riding toward them across the desert. Ran shaded his eyes and studied them closely. He recognized the horses.

"It's Wade Harley and some of my *vaqueros,*" he said. "I figger they're comin' lookin' for me and Angel."

"They'll see that you get back to the ranch all right, won't they?" asked Ray. "If you don't mind,

I think I'd rather turn off here and ride home. Yes, my clothes are dry and I'm all right."

"When'll I see you again?" Ran asked as he slipped to the ground.

"I—I don't know," she replied. "I love Uncle Bruce and I don't want to do anything that would hurt him. Please, wait just a little. Perhaps things will work out."

"All right," Ran told her soberly.

As she rode away, her voice drifted softly back to him:

"But don't wait *too* long, dear!"

Chapter 16
PLANS AND HOPES

OLD Wade listened to Ran's story in silent astonishment:

"Hmmm, so yore *El Cascabel*," he commented when Ran had finished.

"Uh-huh, and you got *El Cascabel's bandidos* ridin' for you."

"Oh, well," said Harley, "I done heerd tell of wuss bandits. And I heerd lots of things 'bout *El Cascabel*, too," he added. "I allus heerd he was a square-shooter even if he was a hell-raiser and I figger whoever he plugged sorta needed pluggin'. How'd you get into sich a mess, son?"

"I was jest trailin' my rope," Ran explained, and told Harley the story of Cal Taylor and the crooked poker game and his flight into Mexico. "Down there," he continued, "I met a lot of fellers in the same fix as me. We got a outfit t'gether and began handin' out a little real justice to the so-called law and order class. *Haciendadoes* who whipped their *peons* to death when they didn't work hard enough, and *alcaldes* who hung poor men jest for the sport of the thing got a taste of their own medicine. Of co'hse they bellered and yelled 'bandit,' 'revolutionary' and other things. Finally the gov'ment sent so many soldiers to run us down I decided we'd better bust up and scatter. I come back to Arizona. I left things a bit cleaner down there.

"Some day," he added prophetically, "a jigger is gonna come along who'll organize the *peons* inter a real army and then there'll be a different kind of Mexico on the map. You watch and see if it don't happen."

Old Wade rode to town the following morning. He came back chuckling and with an astonishing bit of news.

"I can't figger why he done it," he told Ran, "but Bruce Belton went to the sheriff's office yest'day mawnin' and took the county prosecutor along with him. He told the sheriff he didn't have no 'thority to hold you in jail, and to turn you loose. The prosecutor backed him up in it."

Ran was interested. "What'd the sheriff say?" he asked.

Old Wade chuckled louder than ever. "That horned toad's got more gall than a Yaqui buck with a red shirt," he said. "He up and tells Belton that after havin' a talk with you he decided he was in the wrong and had already turned you loose. Can you beat that?"

"How'd he 'splain bein' locked up in his own jail?"

"He didn't, and he waren't locked up when Belton got theah, but that beanpole of a dep'ty of hisn is wearin' a mighty mean grin."

Two days later, while the lanky deputy was "restin'" with his feet on the sheriff's desk, a tall figure strolled in.

"Jest dropped in to get my hat," said Ran Hollis pleasantly.

The deputy did not bat an eye. "Hangin' right there on that peg," he gestured. "Sorry you couldn't stay longer the last time you visited us. Drap in any time yore a mind to."

The following day was payday at the Bar-H. Old Wade handed the grinning Mexicans their high wages and watched them ride off for town.

"Be busted come mawnin'," he commented. "Now, son, let's you and me straighten out our own private accounts. Heah's yore wages, double what I promised you. Hell, you earned 'em! And here," he added, drawing a plump sack from a table drawer, "is what them cattle you grabbed outa that canyon 'long with my herd brought. Shet up, it's yores, ev'ry cent of it. Yeah, I've set a share aside for Angel, but I ain't gonna give it all to him to oncet. If I did he'd corral all the whiskey and *senoritas* in San Salvadore and be dead of 'arithmetism' or somethin' inside of a week!"

Ran "hefted" the sack. "It's a lot of *pesos!*"

Brewster, the San Salvador meat dealer, was yelping for more cattle.

"These damn rock busters 'round here put away more meat than a pack of *lobos*," he told Ran Hollis. "You jest nacherly can't fill 'm up. Prices is risin' all the time, but do they give a damn! Can't you run me another herd in *pronto?* I'm payin' a higher rate than for the last one."

Ran promised, and set to work to get the herd together. With his dark-faced riders, he combed the brakes of the outlying ranges, scoured hidden canyons and hunted strays out of the hills.

The herd grew swiftly. It was corralled a half mile or so from the ranchhouse, where there was shade and water. Ran guarded it carefully against possible fright and stampede.

"Barbed wire won't hold 'em if they happen to start," he cautioned his riders. "They gotta be kept quiet.

"We won't take no chances of another drygulchin' in that damn canyon," he added. "We'll have outriders plenty and send scouts out ahead. We'll put a spoke in *Senor* Winters' wheel if he's figger'n on pullin' another stunt. He's smart, but we'll be smarter."

But Cale Winters was even smarter than most folks gave him credit for. Sitting his horse in the hills to the north, with field glasses to his eyes, he watched the trail herd grow, and made his plans. Devil's Canyon did not figure in them.

Yes, Cale Winters was smart, but not quite smart enough. Not smart enough to see or hear the swarthy little Mexican Ran Hollis had had constantly patrolling the hills since the trail herd began to form. Angel, with Indian stealth and cunning, located the lone watcher. He crept close when Cale Winters was joined by Bert Connors one day. He listened while the two talked earnestly. Then he grinned his wolfish grin and slipped away to warn Ran Hollis.

There came a night of black rainclouds scudding across a hot sky. Heat lightning flickered along the horizon. Far off thunder muttered. Angel, scouting the cleft in the hills through which the trail to the Lazy-B ranch wound, suddenly turned his pony and galloped frantically toward the distant Bar-H. He slammed into the bunkhouse where men sat cleaning and oiling rifles.

"*Capitan*, they come!" he panted. "Even as I said."

"All right," said Ran Hollis quietly. "Let's go, boys."

Inside the big corral was a huddle of dark objects. It looked like a sleeping cattle herd, but it was strangely silent, even for a sleeping herd.

"You think it'll fool 'em?" whispered old Wade

from where he crouched beside Ran in the shadow of a little grove.

"Shore it will," Ran assured him. "They don't suspect nothin'. They'll be lookin' for cattle and that'll make 'em *see* cattle 'stead of a lot of bush tops cut and scattered about. Anyway, we couldn't take a chance with the herd. It would bust loose shore as hell oncet the shootin' started and we couldn't spare any men to handle 'em. They'll be safe in that new corral hid in the canyon."

The night grew even blacker. There was an electric tenseness in the air. Ran felt his nerves tingling, his hair prickling like the hackles on the neck of an angry dog.

"This waitin' and waitin' with nothin' happenin' is hell!" he breathed. "You shore you sighted them, Angel?"

"I am sure, *Capitan*," replied the *vaquero*, "and they are already here. I feel the hoof beats of many horses."

Ran could not sense the slight tremor caused by the advancing hoofs, but he had implicit confidence in Angel's almost uncanny powers of perception. He tensed, gripping his rifle.

"*E-e-e-yow! Crash! Crash! Snappety-crack!*"

Wild yells soared to the black sky. Guns bellowed. Slickers snapped and crackled. Dark shapes flitted about the corral, shooting and whooping.

Cale Winters' voice suddenly lifted in a frantic shout of warning:

"Look out, boys, there ain't nothin' in that corral! It's a trap! Look out!"

From the black shadows of the grove burst a roar of rifle fire. Red flashes slashed the night. Savage yells of triumph arose.

Totally unprepared for such a happening, the raiders went down under the withering blast of lead. Man after man dropped. Some tried to fight back. Others fled, scattering in all directions. The vengeful *vaqueros* leaped to their tethered horses and thundered in pursuit.

"No stoppin' 'em," Ran told old Wade. "They'll never get over what happened in Devil's Canyon. Let's you and me see what we can do for any fellers we find hurt."

They found one, and one only. The concentrated rifle fire had been appallingly deadly. A man was huddled under a bush, moaning with a smashed shoulder and a hole through his leg. They carried him to the ranchhouse and in the light Ran recognized the good looking young cowboy who had sat with Ray Carrol the night she danced.

"Jest a kid," said the big puncher to Harley. "Don't look like a bad sort, either. He's purty much hurt but mebbe we can save him."

They worked over the wounded man for some time, stopped the flow of blood and gave him whiskey and water in small quantities. He gained a little strength and his sufferings seemed somewhat relieved.

"I ain't gonna last long, though," he gasped, "I can feel it." He beckoned to Ran to come closer.

"Feller," he breathed, "I got somethin' to tell you—somethin' I don't wanta take with me on my conscience where I'm goin'. Listen, Cale Winters and the little redhead had one hell of a row today, over you. I thought Winters would shoot her. I b'lieve he would if Belton hadn't stopped him. Belton didn't know anythin' 'bout this raid Winters was plannin', and he don't know that Winters was plannin' on takin' the gal away with him after he got the money for the herd. That's what he was plannin', feller—he was plannin' on stealin' her and carryin' her off. He's got friends in Mexico who will help him hide out or get to South America. He won't wait now. He'll grab her quick as he gets back to the ranch, if he ain't dead, and the chances are he ain't. He was the fust to hightail it. I heerd him and his sidekick, Connors, plannin' the whole thing. You better hustle, feller!"

"Connors is dead," broke in Harley.

Five minutes later Ran Hollis was thundering along the trail to the Lazy-B ranch. He rode his big golden sorrel which had been called "the fastest hoss in all Mexico." He carried his two heavy Colts and there was a rifle snugged in the saddle boot. Eyes bleak, lean jaw tight, he rode, watchful, alert, the great jagged scar on his cheek flaming red.

Overhead the clouds were breaking. Patches of pale sky began to show. Golden spears flung up in the east. The clear air trembled with wonderful tints of mauve and saffron and emerald and rose. In flaming splendor the sun blazed above the eastern peaks. The desert shimmered like myriad gems, a bird flung forth a jewel-burst of song, and it was day.

Through the glory of the morning a lone rider thundered up to the Lazy-B ranchhouse. He flung himself from the saddle and leaped up the wide steps, guns ready, eyes cold as wind-swept ice.

The ranchhouse was strangely silent. Ran hesitated in the hallway, fearing possible ambush. A low babbling sound coming from the big front room brought his guns stabbing toward the half open door. Tense, ready, he glided to the door.

On the floor, his gray hair streaked with blood, lay Bruce Belton. Beside him crouched his terrified Mexican cook. She screamed as she caught sight of Ran.

"Steady, *Senora*," Ran told her. "You ain't gonna be hurt. What happened heah?"

"*Don* Caleb!" gabbled the Mexican woman. "He strike the *patron!* He take *La Senorita* away on his horse! The *patron* fight to save her, but *Don* Caleb strike heem weeth the gun barrel."

Ran knelt beside Belton. "Get some water," he told the cook. *"Pronto! vamos!"*

She brought it, "in a hurry." Ran bathed Belton's temples, sprinkled a little on his face. Belton groaned and opened his eyes.

"Cale!" he growled, "you damn sidewinder! You——"

Suddenly he recognized Ran. With swiftly returning strength he struggled to a sitting position.

"Get after them, Hollis!" he barked. "Save her from that skunk! She loves you, Hollis. That's what the row was about! Get goin', man, yore in shape to ride!"

"Which way'd they go?" Ran urged. "How'm I to foller them?"

"Shadow Canyon trail—it's the only way he can get to Mexico from heah 'thout passin' acrost yore place. That's the road he'll take. Get goin'—don't worry 'bout me. I'm all right 'cept for a headache!"

"Did he hurt her?" asked Ran as he flung erect.

"Nope, I don't think so. He busted the safe and cleaned it and smashed me with his gun. I run in on him jest after he'd finished tiein' her up and gaggin' her. She didn't look hurt."

Shadow Canyon! An evil place of black rock and white water and evil memories. Raiding parties from Mexico ride through it. Stolen cattle go that way to and from the land of *manana*. Bitter battles have been fought there. Men have died terrible deaths in the gloom of its towering walls.

Grim, watchful, deathly tired, Ran Hollis rode into the canyon as the crests of the tall walls were edged with the flame of the setting sun. Already there was much of purple and blue and velvety black at the bottom of the gorge. Night was not far off.

The sorrel's golden coat was dark with sweat and white with flecks of foam. His racing gallop was little more than a shamble; but he slugged his gallant head above the bit and staggered on, nostrils flaring redly, eyes congested with blood.

"Jest a little more, feller," Ran begged, "and mebbe we'll catch up with 'em 'fore dark."

The golden horse snorted understanding and struggled around a craggy bend.

Crash!

Ran saw the glint of the raised rifle a split second before it roared. He was going sideways out of the saddle when Cale Winters pulled trigger. He hit the ground under the sorrel's belly, rolled over and leaped to his feet. Winters' barrel lined with his breast.

Again the rifle boomed, but the black muzzle jerked up the instant before it spouted flame. Ray Carrol, her feet bound securely to her pony's stirrups, had lurched him into Winters' horse and spoiled Cale's aim.

Ran's gun leaped out, but the girl was so close to

Winters he dared not fire. He ran toward the pair,
weaving and ducking. Winters blazed away at him
a third time and cut a lock of dark hair from his
head. He urged his horse forward a few paces,
steadied and took deliberate aim.

Flame and smoke spouted from the muzzle of
Ran's Colt. Winters lurched in the saddle, but he
grimly steadied the rifle barrel. His black eyes
glinted along the sights.

Abruptly one of those terrible, glittering eyes
went blank. Blood poured from it. Winters reeled,
rose in his stirrups and crashed headlong. Ran ran
toward him, gun ready, but there was no need for
another shot. Winters was spilling blood and brains
onto the grass. He was dead when Ran reached
him.

A few slashes of Ran's knife cut Ray loose. He
lifted her to the ground. She clung to him, her
legs too numb to support her weight. Ran gathered
her close in his arms.

"I knew you'd come," she sobbed.

Together they rode to the Lazy-B through the
silvery moonlight. They were very silent. At the
ranchhouse door, Ran set her on her feet. She
stood beside his horse, looking up into his eyes.

"Won't you stay?" she urged.

Ran smiled down at her; then his eyes sobered
and he looked away toward the purple mountains of
Mexico. He was seeing a crippled man with a tired,

lined face—a man whose pride forbade him to accept help from the girl he loved, even though that help meant returned health and strength. He was thinking of Tom Simpson, and of himself. He, Ran Hollis, was, after all, just a penniless cowpoke. All he owned in the world was the horse he bestrode, his guns, and the no great amount of money snugged in the belt that encircled his lean waist beneath his shirt. While the girl who waited expectantly was Bruce Belton's only kin and heiress to the rich Lazy-B and Belton's numerous other properties. No, he couldn't do it! He couldn't ask Ray Carrol to marry him—yet!

Again he smiled down at her. "You'll wait for me, honey?"

The blue eyes were starry with unshed tears, but they met his bravely. "Always," she said, "always and forever!"

Ran said goodbye to Wade Harley, to Angel and the *vaqueros*, and rode north—north toward the great territory of Nevada, which men said was the new land of opportunity. North to the land of silver and gold, of the Overland Stage and the Pony Express.

A magic phrase, that last, the Pony Express. Ran heard much concerning those gay riders of the dim trails, who carried the mails through sunshine and storm, through heat of day and gloom of night, who dared hostile Indians, ruthless outlaws and the hazards of an uncharted course. He watched keenly for a glimpse of the romantic figure that so intrigued his fancy. North he rode, under a sky that seemed eternally blue, through sunlight eternally golden.

Chapter 17

DEATH RIDES

"HERE he comes, hoss!"

Ran Hollis leaned forward in the saddle, his gray eyes shining, a grin of pleased anticipation quirking the corners of his wide, good-humored mouth. His lean, sinewy body tensed in sympathy with the oncoming rider. Under his thin shirt the muscles of back and shoulder and arm swelled and rippled. The big golden sorrel snorted a protest as Ran's thighs tightened against his ribs. The cowboy relaxed with a chuckle.

"Guess I'm ridin' right with him," he told the sorrel. "Boy, see him go!"

On came the rider, rising and falling, rising and falling—sweeping toward the tall young puncher who sat his horse on the crest of a little knoll—growing more and more distinct and more and more sharply defined. The flutter of hoofs came distinctly to Ran's ear. He could hear the explosive breathing of the flying horse. There was the wave of a hand, a quick-fire drum of wafer-thin iron shoes and horse and man were past the cowboy and winging away like a belated fragment of a storm.

So swift and vanishing, so utterly unreal in the vast solitude of empty prairie and empty sky, that were it not for a flake of white foam quivering and perishing amid the green sway of a tuft of grass, Ran might have doubted that he had actually watched the Pony Express flash by.

The cowboy breathed deeply. "Hoss," he said, "next to bein' a tophand with a good cow outfit, I callate theah ain't anythin' goin' I'd rather be than a pony-rider. If we don't find us another job of cow chambermaidin' 'fore long, mebbe *we* can get a job carryin' the mails. Co'hse I'm sorta sizeable for that bus'ness, but you never can tell, hoss, you never can tell."

He chuckled with amusement at the idea—six-footers who weighed around 190 pounds in overalls were not exactly the proper material for pony-riders.

"He rides fifty miles without restin'," continued the cowboy, his eyes still on the fleeting figure. "Ev'ry ten miles or so he hell-whoops up to a station, hops onto a fresh hoss that's standin' all ready, and away he goes! He—*hell's-fire!*"

Ran suddenly saw the distant horse go hurtling end over end through the air. The puncher could sense the crash of the fall he could not hear. He saw the black dot that was the rider strike the ground and bounce drunkenly. The dot became a motionless huddle beside the motionless horse. To Ran's ear drifted the faint, whiplash crack of a rifle. He went into instant action.

"Get goin', hoss!" he barked, driving his knees against the sorrel's sides.

Down the knoll thundered the great golden gelding, his coat flashing in the sunlight, his red nostrils flaring. He had been champing impatiently ever since that other "thoroughbred" had flitted past him. Now he stretched his mighty legs, hugged his belly to the ground and fled across the flower dotted prairie like the shadow of a star before a lightning flash. Ran Hollis, grim of jaw and hard of eye, urged him to greater efforts of speed.

Ran did not know what it was all about, but he *did* know that murder had just been done before his eyes and he knew that more crooked work was in the making.

"Theah comes the hellion!" he gritted between set teeth. "He's after somethin', sho' as blazes. Do it, hoss! do it! Get me clost enough to line sights on the sidewinder jest once! Sift sand, hoss!"

From behind a rocky hillock a single horseman had dashed. He raced toward the fallen pony-rider, bending low in the saddle and heaving his shoulders as if he were lifting his horse at each stride. He reached the silent figure on the ground before the galloping cowboy was within long pistol range. Ran saw him pull his bronk to a sliding halt, hurl himself from the saddle and kneel beside the motionless mail carrier. His hands moved swiftly, surely. There was a sudden flash of white and the dry-gulcher leaped erect again and swung into the saddle.

Ran jerked his right-hand gun and let drive. It was long shooting for a six—even for the long-bar-reled single-action Colts the cowboy carried in their carefully worked and oiled quick-draw holsters. Ran had little hope of scoring a hit. He whooped with delight as a sudden howling curse flung back at him from the drygulcher.

"Winged him, sho' as hell!" he exulted as some-thing white went swirling and fluttering through the air—a fragment of the sheet of paper the other was stuffing into his belt.

The drygulcher whirled his horse and jerked a rifle from the saddle boot. Ran thumbed the ham-mer of his Colt desperately. Smoke and flame streamed from the black muzzle. The reports were a staccato drum roll. Then the rifle roared.

Even before he heard the sullen thud of the strik-ing bullet, Ran knew the drygulcher had scored. A pang of anguish, worse than if the big slug had ripped through his own flesh, knifed his heart as the sorrel screamed in agony. Down went the golden horse, in a sprawling kicking heap, and over his head went Ran. He struck with a crash, twitched and lay still, blood pouring from a nasty gash just above his right temple. The drygulcher glared for an instant with burning black eyes, mouthed a curse and wrung his fingers that dripped blood where Ran's bullet had creased them. Then he whirled his horse again and rode swiftly into the red eye of the setting sun.

Chapter 18

THE DEVIL'S OWN

THE sun had set and the western sky was ablaze with scarlet and gold and turkis-green when Ran Hollis groaned, writhed and sat up. He was sick and dizzy and for a moment his mind was utterly blank to what had happened. Then memory returned with a rush and he cursed feebly. He passed a shaking hand across his aching head, stared at his reddened fingers and swore some more. He got to his feet and stood swaying.

His horse was dead—a glance told him that. Dead also was the horse of the pony-rider. Ran walked unsteadily to the silent form of the man.

"He's dead, too," he muttered after a brief examination. "Fall busted his neck. Helluva wonder the one I took didn't bust mine! That blankety-blank-blank so-and-so knows how to handle a long gun, all right, and he's ornery enough to aim at a hoss 'stead of a man. Well, I marked him, and I got a good look at his pig eyes and cinch-ring of a mouth 'fore I took that header. I'll know him if I ever run acrost him again, and when I do——"

171

The tightening of the puncher's thin lips and the bleak glare in his green-gray eyes finished a threat that was really not a threat, but a promise.

Ran looked the pony-rider over before the light failed completely. He was a thin little wisp of a man with a face and eyes that must have been merry in life. His dress was thin and fitted close—a skull-cap, a "round-about," pantaloons tucked into boot tops. He carried no arms, and nothing else not absolutely necessary. He hardly would, with the postage on his literary freight worth *five dollars a letter!* He strove for the irreducible minimum of weight.

The horse wore a little wafer of a racing saddle and no visible blanket. The little flat mail-pockets were still strapped in place. Ran stared at them, a perplexed crease between his eyes.

"What was that hellion after?" he wondered. "If he didn't bother the mail I'm sho' he took somethin'—I saw it in his hand—but what? Pony-riders don't carry no money or nothin' wuth stealin'. How come this pore devil to get drygulched, anyhow? It don't make sense."

He glanced about, as if seeking the solution from the rolling range land, now purple and mysterious in the blue dusk, and his eye caught a flutter of white against a clump of sage.

It was a torn fragment of airily thin paper. Ran could just make out words written in watery ink.

He struck a match and by its feeble glow spelled out the words—

"Taylor's going to kill . . . runs Arivapa . . . county . . . get word . . . without help . . . rich . . ."

Where the corner of the fragment jagged away, Ran read a portion of a name—"Whitmer."

As the match burned his fingers, Ran dropped it to the ground and carefully stamped it out. He thoughtfully creased the paper fragment and put it in an inside pocket, shaking his head the while.

"Arivapa," he mused, "that's the town I'm headin' for, and 'cordin' to what folks have told me of late, I oughta be gettin' purty close to it. And it seems plumb nacherel and homelike to find Cal Taylor's name mixed up in some skullduggery 'fore I'm even in smellin' distance of his hangout.

"That chunk of paper I picked up, now, it looks like it might be part of a letter. Guess my bullet ripped it loose from the whole sheet that sidewinder was stuffin' in his belt when I pulled trigger. If I had the rest of it, mebbe I could figger things out; but I ain't got it. All I got is one helluva haidache and a darn good chance of starvin' to death 'fore I hit some place where there's grub. I callate I got jest about enough left for one more swallerin'. Guess mebbe I'd better whack it in half and save some for t'morrer. Fust thing, though, I'll cover this pore feller with rocks so the coyotes won't get him. Chances are some of his bunkies'll come lookin' for what's left of him when he don't show up at the next station."

Dry sagebrush provided wood for a fire. Ran had his old fryingpan and a battered coffee pot in his saddlebags. He cooked a scanty meal, spread his blankets and slept several hours. The stars were still golden jewels in the diadem of night when he rolled cooking utensils and his meagre food supply in the blankets and hoisted the pack to his shoulders. He cast a regretful glance at his saddle, but that hull weighed around forty pounds.

"Which is a hulluva lot too much to be amblin' 'round through these darn hills and gullies with," Ran decided. "Mebbe I can come back and get her oncet I get located—if the coyotes don't chaw it all up fust. Now which way to go? That drygulcher went west, so guess I'll jest go west, too. That's the gen'ral d'rection I'm travellin' in, anyhow."

The golden stars paled to silver and vanished. The fairy fingers of the dawn traced the eastern sky with rose and mauve and shimmering amethyst. The western mountain peaks flashed golden. A blue ripple of wind walked across the prairie grasses, a bird sang, the sun thundered up over the edge of the world, and it was day.

"Gonna be a scorcher, too," predicted Ran as he trudged on toward those distant mountains now hard and clear-cut and gray against the brassy western sky.

Three days later, gaunt and famished, with black beard stubbling his hollow cheeks, he toiled up a last long rise and stood for a moment staring at a sprawling huddle and a dark smudge that crawled along a flank of one of those gray mountains.

The sprawling huddle was the houses of a good sized town. The smudge was the smoke that rolled up from the chimneys of stamp mill and shop and engine house.

"Looks like a hell-buster, too," commented Ran. "Ev'thing new, ev'thing busy. One of them gold-strike towns what's been boomin' up in these Nevada hills of late. Anyhow, betcha theah's somethin' to eat theah!"

Another hour's walking brought him to the town. It was a real one, all right, and business was evidently booming—business of various sorts. Ran could hear the hollow rumble of blasts being set off in the bowels of the mountain. In his ears dinned the thundering clatter of the stamp mills. Machinery whined and clanked. The streets were choked with ore wagons and mules and horses. Ran's eyes brightened as he headed for a sign that said, "Restaurant."

"Keep'er comin' till I tell you to stop," he ordered the Chinese cook. "I got lots of space what needs fillin'. You take a bite fust, though, and let me watch you. I ain't et for so long I done forgot how to chaw!"

"Can do," smiled the cook. "You likum heap plenty glub? Can do."

Ran ate until the cook forgot his English and marvelled in Chinese that sounded like fire crackers exploding in a jug. Finally the puncher shoved back his chair, rolled a cigarette and puffed with deep satisfaction.

"You take care of my bedroll till I look up a place to pound my ear?" he asked the cook. "I wanta get a shave and a drink fust."

"Can do," agreed the Chinaman heartily. "Cook more glub when you come back. Bobble shop right next door."

A little later, his bronzed cheeks appearing somewhat thinned, even after a shave, but with the brightness back in his eyes and the spring in his step, Ran Hollis ambled up the crowded main street of the mining town. Twilight was shrouding the mountain with robes of royal purple and lamps were casting golden bars of radiance across the board sidewalk.

"She's salty, all right," declared the puncher. "Ev'ry other place a saloon, dancehall or gamblin' joint. And them places with the purty red lights ain't no churches, either. Well, here goes for a little dust washer."

He entered a saloon from which light poured and music blared. The slither of cards, the click of

roulette wheels and the stamp and patter of dancing
feet added a cheerful undertone. Song, or what
passed for it, bellowed up to the big hanging lamps
that blazed redly in a blue murk of tobacco smoke.

"Whiskey," Ran told a perspiring barkeep, one
of a battery of drink jugglers that squirmed and
monkey-motioned back of the "mahogany" like pack
rats in a cactus patch.

The barkeep deftly knocked the neck off a bottle
and sloshed a water glass full of "red likker." Ran
downed it, drew a deep breath and reached for the
bottle.

" 'Nother one for a chaser," he said, "and then
I'll take the next one sorta easy."

The barkeep blinked at the "white" showing in
the quart bottle.

"Next one's on the house," he stated emphatically.
"Any feller what can down two glasses of that hand-
runnin' is sho' entitled to one free. How'd you like
'er?"

"Not bad," Ran admitted. "Sorta mild, though."

"Mild!"

The barkeep gagged and sputtered. "Dad-blame
you!" he gasped, "you made me swaller my chaw!
Mild!"

Glass in hand, Ran leaned against the bar and
watched the dancers. The men were mostly miners
in blue woolen shirts and pantaloons stuffed into
boots. There was a sprinkling of cow punchers and

a few tight-lipped individuals in black coats. Gamblers and dealers off duty, these last, Ran surmised.

"Gals don't look so bad," mused the cowboy, "'specially after a coupla drinks."

The girls were young, with trim figures. But their eyes, for the most part, were calculating and their painted lips lacked softness. Their partners took small note of deficiencies, however. They whirled the girls about with wild abandon, whooping in time to the music, stamping the sanded floor. One big fellow with bushy black whiskers did a solo, jig-time, as the booming strains of "Buffalo Gals" boiled from fiddle and banjo and guitar.

"Ridin' high, wide and handsome!" chuckled Ran. "Say, this ain't a one half bad *pueblo!* I've seen a lot wuss towns."

He turned to the bar and refilled his empty glass. "What's the name of this burg?" he asked the bartender.

"We calls her Arivapa," said the barkeep. "Don't ask me why, 'cause I'm damned if I know."

Two men came through the swinging doors and walked toward the corner of the room where tables and chairs were provided for weary customers or those who had taken on more than their tonnage. Ran Hollis, his hat pulled low, eyed them with interest, the jagged scar on his cheek burning darkly red.

Both men were big, but with a different bigness. One was beefy and solid with a square red face, a

gripping mouth and arrogant ice-blue eyes. He
walked with the assured tread of a man who is a
master of material things. His huge hands were
balled into fists and they gave the impression that
they were habitually that way. His clothes were
rough and showed much service, but he wore them
as a captain-general wears uniform.

The other man was tall and rangy, with a dead
white face and eyes that were like pools of ink with
fire burning beneath them. He glided rather than
walked and his bony hands dangled loosely beside his
thighs and close to the big blue guns sagging there.
He was a shivery sort—the kind that evoluted from
the snake rather than from the monkey.

The two men brushed through the dancers as if
they were not on the floor. Ran noticed that the
couples gave way to them without argument. He
wondered what was back of that purposeful march
across the room.

The men halted before a table at which sat a lone
man, an inoffensive sort of person with mild eyes.
A little man, Ran noted, with a bowed back. He
was not old. His chin, square and resolute, belied
the mild eyes.

The beefy man leaned across the table and said
something Ran could not catch. The seated man
glanced up and did not reply at once. Then he
slowly shook his head. Ran saw the big man's lips
writhe back in a wolfish snarl. He seemed to spit

words through clenched teeth. The other stared an instant and leaped to his feet. He swung an awkward blow at the big man's face. The big man stepped back, and as the musicians finished a fandango in an abrupt crash of chords, Ran heard his rasping voice——

"Whitmer, you been told plenty. Now you're gonna get it!"

His huge fist shot out and hurled the slighter man to the floor. Then he and the bony man started kicking the huddled form to bits.

It was not Ran's fight, and really none of his business. But the cold brutality of the affair sickened the cowboy and sent a red wave of rage boiling through his brain. He went across the room like a bronze streak.

The beefy man saw him coming, but not soon enough. He had half turned and was bringing his guard up when Ran struck. The puncher's fist thudded against the other's jaw like a butcher's cleaver on a side of beef.

The big man went down, taking a table, two chairs and a fine assortment of bottles and glassware with him. Ran slewed around and let his bony companion have one that started from the floor. *He* landed in the midst of the orchestra with his head through a banjo and two cursing musicians sprawled across his middle.

The beefy man came up again, reeking blood,

spilled whiskey and blue-black profanity. With a wordless roar he rushed.

Ran ducked under the flailing arms and grasped the other about the thighs. His wide shoulders heaved mightily, his back straightened.

Over his head went the beefy man, arms and legs revolving wildly. He hit the floor with a crash that jarred the building and lay moaning and writhing, all the breath knocked out of him.

Crash!

Ran felt the wind of the passing bullet before he heard the six-gun's roar. He slewed sidewise as the bony man threw down for another shot.

That one knocked a back-bar mirror to splinters and at the same instant Ran's right hand flickered down and up.

Ran didn't intend to make a spectacular play—he aimed at the "thickest" part—but the bony man's gun hand got in the way. The heavy slug from Ran's Colt knocked his gun spinning and took a good part of his thumb with it. He screeched with rage and pain and clawed at his left-hand holster. His fingers curled around the black gun butt, and froze as Ran's voice bit at him, edged with steel——

"Do it and shake hands with the Devil! All right, elevate, pronto!

"Stay wheah you are, you!" he flung at the beefy man, who was struggling to rise. His green eyes, cold now as winter ice, swept the milling crowd.

A hush fell at that bleak glare. Men shuffled their feet and held their hands rigid. Each felt that those icy eyes and those black gun muzzles were singling him out for individual attention.

"Anybody else got a int'rest in this shindig?" Ran asked softly. "Huh? Now's the time to get goin' if you have."

The silence persisted until a big miner, the one who had soloed the jig, sang out:

"Ain't none of our affair, cowboy. We come heah to drink and dance, not to ketch lead pizenin'."

Ran nodded. His guns stabbed at the two big men. "All right, you two, get goin'. Trail outa here, *pronto,* and if you come back 'fore I leave, come smokin'. *Sabe?*"

Stiffly the big beefy man got to his feet. He glared at Ran, amazed recognition filming the rage and hatred in his eyes.

"H-Hollis!" he stuttered. "By God! are yuh allus gonna be tanglin' yore rope in my affairs?"

"Looks sorta that way, don't it, Cal," returned the cowboy imperturbably. "Perhaps if yuh ever tried walkin' a straight trail for a change, things'd be different."

Cal Taylor spoke thickly, seeming to get the words out with difficulty:

"You got by with it this time, but it ain't finished. Next time——"

He turned his back on the cowboy and limped to

the swinging doors, lunged them open with his shoulders and vanished. His companion followed him, dead-white face expressionless again, but Ran saw his spear-head hands, one dripping blood, writhe and coil like constricting snakes.

Chapter 19

WATER AND WAR

RAN holstered his guns and turned to the bar as talk roared up from the crowded dance floor. The bartender regarded him solemnly.

"Have another one on the house," offered that individual. "You gotta drink fast and often from now on, if yore gonna get anythin' like your share."

"What you mean?" Ran asked wonderingly.

"Jest this," said the barkeep, pouring a brimming glass, "any jigger what locks horns with Cal Taylor, to say nothin' of that gun slingin', shootin'-in-the-back bodyguard of hisn, Bat Munson, ain't for long in this here old vale of cryin' and laughin' and aggravatin' women. Drink fast, cowboy, and often!"

Ran grinned at him, then he repeated—"Taylor? I know I—sufferin' sandtoads!"

Before his eyes suddenly drifted words scrawled on a fragment of thin paper—"Taylor—Arivapa." And then, like an echo to the big man's rasping snarl—"Whitmer!"

184

"Say—" he began, and turned as a hand touched his arm.

At his elbow stood the little mild man, wiping blood from his face. He looked Ran in the eyes.

"Thanks," he said simply.

Ran grinned down at him.

The little man smiled, but his eyes were serious.

"You saved me from death or serious injury," he declared. "They would have killed or crippled me before they got through. Me striking at Taylor gave them all the excuse they needed."

"What about this here Taylor?" Ran asked curiously.

The little man's smile grew bitter. His mild eyes flashed:

"He's a murderer and a thief, and everything else a man shouldn't be. He owns the Mescalero mine and he owns this town, or thinks he does. Hardly anyone dares argue the question with him."

"Mescalero mine a big one?" Ran asked.

"Biggest here," nodded the little man. "Biggest and richest. He has an interest in one or two others, also, but the Mescalero is the important one. It employs five hundred men and gives Taylor power to do just about as he pleases."

He eyed Ran speculatively as the puncher downed his drink. He spoke with sudden decision:

"Come over to my cabin with me, won't you.

I'll tell you the whole story. Perhaps you'll find it interesting."

Ran gave him a quick look, and nodded agreement.

"All right. I am sorta curious, I admit. Seems theah's all kinds of funny doin's goin' on in this *pueblo*. I wanta stop at that restaurant down the street a minute, fust. Chink what owns it is keepin' my bedroll for me."

The little man started to push the swinging doors apart. Ran gripped him by the shoulder and jerked him back.

"Hold it!" snapped the cowboy. "You don't know what's outside them doors. Listen, now— we'll go through t'gether, fast. I'll slew to the right and you slew to the left—damn fast. Don't bobble it!"

Through the doors they went, slamming them back on their hinges, and slithered along the wooden side of the building.

Wham!

A slug ripped through the flimsy boards scant inches from Ran's head. From inside the saloon sounded a yell of pain and anger. Ran went headlong behind a hitchpost, guns coming out. He saw the blaze of the drygulcher's gun in a dark opening between two buildings across the street. Both his own guns let go in a rippling crash as feet thudded down the alley. Weaving and ducking he raced across the street; but the alley was empty when he reached it. He holstered his guns and went back to the small man, who was still flattened against the side of the building.

"Jest a little game of tag me and a feller was playing'," Ran told the gathering crowd. "C'mon, Whitmer, that's yore name, ain't it?"

Whitmer's cabin was small, but strongly constructed and comfortably furnished. It sat in the mouth of a fairly wide draw on the northern outskirts of the town. Glancing about, Ran saw evidence of another occupant besides his host.

"Them things belonged to my dad," said Whitmer, interpreting the glance. "He's dead now."

"Been daid long?" Ran asked sympathetically.

"Three days!"

"Three days!"

"Uh-huh, shot three days ago; buried him yest'day."

Ran shook his head. "Any idea who shot him?"

Whitmer shrugged and his mouth was hard and bitter.

" 'Party or parties unknown,' the coroner's jury said. Of course I know damn well that Cal Taylor was back of it, but I can't prove anythin'. Wouldn't do much good if I could, in this town."

He held up his hand. "Listen," he said.

Ran listened. From the darkness of the draw came a musical purl and chatter.

"That," said Whitmer, "is what's behind all this trouble."

"Sounds like a crik," Ran wondered. "How could a crik get yore dad killed and you darn neah it?"

"Water causes plenty killin's in this country," said Whitmer. "This is a mighty dry section and water is valuable."

"It's caused plenty of trouble on range land," Ran admitted, "but you ain't raisin' cattle here."

"Water is just as important to minin' as it is to cattle," said Whitmer. "You can't get along without it. Here's what happened——

"Dad homesteaded this section long before there were any mines. The land in the draw is good land. Also there is a whoopin' big spring at the head of the draw. Ownin' the draw, Dad naturally owned the spring. Along came the gold and silver strikes. Cal Taylor was one of the first here. He got control of what is now the Mescalero mine. He needed water bad to run that big mine—more water than he had on his land—so he made a deal with Dad. He traded Dad a claim that was once part of the Mescalero for half his water. Dad built a dam just above the mouth of the draw and diverted half the stream so that Taylor could run it into his ditches."

"Why couldn't Taylor tap it after the stream left the draw?" asked Ran.

"Stream doesn't leave the draw," said Whitmer. "Just above the mouth of the draw it drops into a hole and goes plumb outa sight. Never comes up again. So long as we own the draw we completely control the water. Taylor knows that."

"And without the water the Mescalero ain't no good?"

"Just about that," Whitmer admitted.

" 'Pears like Taylor woulda wanted to keep yore dad friendly 'stead of gettin' him on the prod," commented Ran.

"Uh-huh, he did—until that claim he traded Dad turned out to be 'bout the richest part of the Mescalero. Leastwise it looks that way. It isn't fully developed yet. Taylor is money mad, and mad for power. He's increased his influence until he just about runs things around here. He thinks that everything oughta belong to him and he figgers Dad did him wrong in that trade. I guess he thought the claim was worthless when he traded it. He tried to get Dad to give him back a half interest and when Dad refused he got ugly and started trouble. We didn't have much money and because of Taylor's opposition we haven't been able to develop the claim much. He told Dad he would never be able to develop it and when Dad told him he was gonna get help from outside Arivapa, Taylor blew up and threatened him if he tried it. I don't know for sure whether Dad tried or not, but somebody killed him."

Ran nodded gravely. "Uh-huh, I'm purty shore he tried, all right."

"What you mean?" demanded Whitmer.

Ran fumbled out the fragment of paper he had found beside the dead pony-rider and handed it to Whitmer.

"That yore dad's writin'?" he asked.

"It is," replied Whitmer after a quick glance. "Where'd you get it?"

Ran told him the whole story. Whitmer nodded, his jaw setting grimly.

"I knew that pony-rider," he said when Ran had finished. "His name was Bert Rappold. Him and Dad were close friends. There's a Pony Express station about six miles due north of here. Dad musta rode up there and give Bert that letter. Evidently Taylor knew what Dad was up to and had one of his paid killers drygulch Bert so the letter wouldn't be delivered. That letter was goin' to Salt Lake City. Dad had a brother there, Peter Whitmer, who is a big man with the Mormons and a friend of Brigham Young. Dad knew Uncle Pete would help him. Taylor knew it, too."

"Won't he help you?" Ran asked.

Whitmer shook his head.

"I don't think so. Uncle Pete never had any

use for me. He's a swashbucklin' hell-fire fighter and I have never been that kind. Dad sent me east to the States, to school, and when I came back here I didn't even talk like a westerner—hardly do now—and that finished me with Uncle Pete. He would have done anything for Dad, but I doubt if he'd raise his hand to help me."

"Which sorta puts you up against it, eh?" commented Ran.

"Yes," said Whitmer bitterly, "and that's why I asked you to come to my cabin. I don't even know your name, but you pulled me outa a bad hole tonight and doin' it you showed all the fightin' qualities and things I haven't got. All I have is a mine that may be worth a lot of money. I'm makin' you the proposition that you throw in with me and we'll share the mine fifty-fifty.

"Don't forget, though," he added hastily before Ran could speak, "you'll be takin' over more than your share of the trouble. I know my limitations. If things go bad and get rough, mebbe I won't be much help to you."

Ran grinned down at the little man and his eyes were green and warm as sun-drenched sea water.

"Feller," he drawled, "you got somethin' what lots of good fightin' men ain't got over much of— two somethin's, in fact. You got guts and you got the habit of tellin' the truth 'bout things, yoreself included, and them somethin's go a long way. I'm a cow puncher, not a miner, and theah's lots about minin' I don't know, but I know somethin' and I can learn more. When Taylor or one of his hellions tried to drygulch me t'night, he made a puhsonal issue outa this bus'ness with me. Feller, we'll jest shake hands on that prop'sition."

"And have a drink on it," grinned Whitmer, hauling a quart bottle from beneath his bunk.

"Mebbe this's the chance I'm lookin' for," Ran told himself as he went to sleep to dream of blue eyes, and hair like a forest pool brimful of sunset.

Chapter 20

LEAD AND GOLD

RAN slept in a comfortable bunk and woke up hungry. While Whitmer prepared breakfast in the lean-to kitchen back of the cabin, Ran stood at the open window and gazed at the crest of the cliff that walled in the draw.

"Sho' is a purty place," he mused, his eyes fixed on the line of saffron flame where the light of early morning poured over the cliff edge. "It oughta be a—what the——?"

His keen eyes had caught a sudden sparkling glint up there on the cliff top. The glint shifted slightly and as it did so Ran hurled himself away from the window.

Whe-e-e-e-e! *Slam!*

Something screeched through the window and smacked loudly into the opposite wall. Ran rolled over and over and dived for the door leading to the lean-to. Whitmer shouted startled inquiry.

"Got a rifle?" Ran barked. "Hustle!"

He took the "long gun" Whitmer jerked from its supporting pegs, crouched to the window and rested the slim barrel across the ledge. He cuddled his cheek against the walnut stock and waited.

Whitmer, peering through the lean-to door, saw the puncher's gray-green eyes, now utterly cold and hard as agates, glance along the sights. He saw the bronzed left hand tighten on the grip as Ran, catching again that almost imperceptible glint on the cliff top, squeezed the trigger. Blueish smoke spurted from the rifle's muzzle and its whiplash crack rang through the cabin. Ran Hollis stood erect and gazed steadily at the light-crowned crest.

He saw a dark form suddenly jerk up, poise for an instant on the dizzy edge and then bend slowly forward. Down, down, rushed the figure, turning wildly in the air, arms and legs flapping brokenly. With a crash plainly audible to the cold-eyed listener it struck the ground at the base of the cliff. Ran's lazy drawl reached the horrified Whitmer:

"There's one buzzard what won't roost on rocks no more. Let's go and see what kinda feathers he's got."

They found the mangled corpse lying sprawled amid a jumble of rock fangs. Ran glanced at the glazing black eyes and the cruel, loose-lipped mouth and nodded his satisfaction.

"What'd you say that pore pony-rider feller's name was?" he asked Whitmer. "Well, yore friend Rappold oughta rest sorta easier now, seein' as the sidewinder what cashed him in is ridin' the toe of

the Devil's boot inter the hottest corner the Old
Boy's got vacant right at present. Yeah, it's him
all right; I got a good look at him jest 'fore he
plugged my hoss. Now if the horned toad what
did for yore dad'll jest come nosin' around."

Whitmer's face was white, his eyes hot with
memory.

"That's how they killed Dad," he said. "I found
him on the cabin floor with a hole 'tween his eyes.
Mebbe it was this dead scoundrel that did it."

"Mebbe," Ran admitted, "but I doubt it. Rappold was killed 'bout forty miles east of heah, best
I can figger. Chances are this feller was holed up
out theah in them rocks waitin' for him for quite a
while. He'd hardly shoot yore dad heah in Arivapa
and then ride way out theah on the prairie the same
day. Nope, I callate we got us another rock rooster
to look out for. One thing's sho', we're gonna
board that window up."

On their way to the mine, Whitmer pointed out
the dam which divided the stream.

"There goes Taylor's water," he said. "It runs
'round that little hill and then he's got sluices to
carry it to his tanks and engine houses. Ours runs
this way after it supplies our water wheel. See
where it drops into the ground? I wish I could
figure some way to make it run to the town, but it
just don't seem possible."

Ran gazed into the black chasm that swallowed the creek. Its depth was evidently enormous, for the wide and deep stream dropped into it absolutely without sound other than the sibilant hiss of the water against the rocky lip. Darkly green and frothily white, the liquid column sank out of sight in the utter gloom, with no answering roar welling up from the depths.

The thing was weird and uncanny and the effect on a watcher was tremendous. Ran found himself leaning farther and farther over the lip of the sink. He jerked back and a film of moisture broke out on his forehead, despite the dankly cold draft that rushed up from the chasm.

"Whew! what a hole!" he exclaimed. "Betcha the Chinamen on the other side the world are usin' this water to sprinkle clothes with. I got a notion she slides right on through without stoppin'. Sho' would hate to drop in theah. Let's be steppin' along to the mine."

Whitmer had a couple of dozen men working for him, all he could afford to pay. They had sunk a shaft to a good depth and were tunneling through the lode.

"It sure looks promising," he told Ran; "better than the top drifts of the Mescalero ever have. Of course we are little more than making expenses right now and the stamp mill we built—that's it over there against the cliff—ran us heavily in debt, but the deeper we go the richer the ore should get. If things work out like they oughta, we'll soon be on easy street."

"I got a notion they ain't gonna work so easy, though," Ran replied. "Cal Taylor is the kinda *hombre* what don't know when he's packed a lickin'. He's salty and he ain't bothered with no sich little thing as a conscience. Jest wait till he learns you and me is tied up t'gether. He'll throw a fit, and he'll make us throw one if we don't watch out."

All that day Ran prowled through the gloomy drifts of the mine, with Whitmer pointing out and explaining. Once the cowboy paused and listened intently. Seeping apparently from the solid rock wall of the tunnel came a faint ghostly tapping.

"What's that?" he asked Whitmer. "Devils locked up in that rock?"

Whitmer chuckled. "Sounds like it, doesn't it? Some of 'em may be devils, all right, but they're not locked up. What you're hearin' is the picks of the miners in one of the Mescalero drifts. Their lode runs mighty close to ours in places."

"Ain't they liable to come bustin' through inter our mine some day?" Ran asked.

"They might," Whitmer admitted, "but it wouldn't matter. They can only follow their vein; they can't touch ours. If their vein ran right across ours they would have a perfect right to follow it— that's mining law—but there wouldn't be any mistaking our vein for theirs. The rock is totally different. An old resident in a mining camp can look at a mixed pile of rock, separate the fragments and tell you right off hand which mine each came from. The Mescalero wouldn't gain anything by breaking into our mine. Claim jumping is just a little too raw for even Cal Taylor to attempt, even in Arivapa. The miners would be organizing a vigilant committee in a hurry. No, what we've got to look out for is something underhand."

Chapter 21

THE RED DESTROYER

THAT night Ran and Whitmer went to town.

"I been amblin' 'round over open range so long I darn neah forgot what likker tastes like," Ran chuckled. "And I'd like to play me a few hands of poker, too."

"I'll go along and watch," agreed Whitmer. "I don't drink much and I'm afraid of girls, and I don't know how to play poker, but I like to watch the crowd."

Ran grinned down at his diminutive partner. "Sometimes I plumb sympathize with yore Uncle Pete," he declared. "Feller, you jest gotta acquire yoreself a few bad habits."

Whitmer laughed good humoredly. "Maybe I will," he said. "Uncle Pete would let you scramble eggs in his Sunday hat. You'd sure fit into his idea of things as they oughta be. Say, things are lively down here tonight. Guess it's payday for the Mescalero."

It was, and Arivapa was celebrating. Saloon and dancehall and gambling den and brothel blazed

199

with light. The streets were a riot of color where
miner and cowboy and prospector jostled one
another. "Civilized" Indians from the prairies
stalked by wrapped in red or blue or yellow blankets,
their black eyes glinting but their faces otherwise
expressionless. Here and there a Chinaman, his
yellow face glowing golden in the lamplight, pat-
tered along with flapping trousers and dangling
pigtail. A Negro, black as original sin, with white
teeth showing in a merry grin, attracted considerable
attention.

"That darky sho' has got hisself a long ways
from home," Ran chuckled. "Looks like he might
be hungry."

He slipped a silver dollar into the colored man's
pink palm and showed teeth white as the darky's
own in a friendly smile.

"Feller," said Whitmer, "when you grin that
way and your eyes light up, you'd bring dogs and
horses and kids runnin' to you.

"And I'd just as soon have a rattlesnake look me
in the eyes when you're on the prod about somethin'," he added under his breath.

A barker stood before a big saloon, bellowing at
the top of his voice:

"Walk in, gents! walk in! The best whiskey and
the purtiest gals in town! You don't hafta b'lieve
me when I tell you that whiskey's prime! Jest
read the label on the bottle—it speaks for itself;

and the gals can do their own talkin', too. And, gents, can they hoof it! One drink and one dance and yore liable to blow yore brains out—theah jest ain't anythin' more left to live for! Take a chance, gents! Music and dancin' and straight games!"

"Wonder if he's lyin'?" Ran chuckled. "Let's go in and see."

They found plenty of whiskey that tasted like a Roman candle procession going through a powder factory. The dancing girls, gay in their bright silks and spangles, looked very well under lamplight, and the gambling games appeared no crookeder than usual. The music, sobbing from the strings of violins and guitars that vibrated beneath the deft touch of dark Mexican fingers, was really good. Ran enjoyed it more than he did whiskey, girls or poker.

"That singin' jigger could make a Apache buck beller tears as big as aigs outa his ears," he told Whitmer. "Jest listen at him!"

> "Love, hear the night wind
> Sobbing beneath the stars!"

The dark-faced orchestra leader had a voice like sun-golden rain falling on swaying roses, and he knew how to use it:

> "Love, heed the kiss of the moonlight
> Upon your cheeks!"

Miners with porcupine whiskers bristling to the four winds tried to look soulful. Gamblers tried to look human. A bartender wept in a glass of whiskey and swallowed it, tears and all. The singer choked on his own emotions and wondered if he would get his pay raised.

"Let's have somethin' quick and devilish!" whooped a cowboy.

"Buffalo gals, ain't you comin' out t'night?"

Lustily the dancers took up the chorus. The roof beams trembled to the rousing old frontier song roared out in a half dozen keys.

"Reminds me of a time I heard seven Scotch bag-pipers in a little room all playin' different chunes," commented the barkeep. "Gosh, that was heavenly!"

"Here comes somethin' what ain't," remarked Ran Hollis.

Into the hilarious room strode Cal Taylor, the white-faced Bat Munson at his heels as usual. Ran noted that Munson's right hand was bandaged.

Taylor favored Ran with a single cold glare and then directed his attention to Whitmer. Munson ignored him entirely. Ran slouched comfortably, back against the bar, and rolled a cigarette.

"Whitmer," said Taylor, "I'm makin' you a last offer, and it ain't a bad one—will you sell?"

Whitmer slowly shook his head.

"I haven't the whole say any more, Taylor," he replied quietly. "You'd hafta get my partner's consent before I could do anything. I'm leavin' everything up to him. This is him, Ran Hollis."

For a moment Ran thought Taylor was going to suffer a stroke. His face turned purple, his eyes bulged. His breath seemed to curdle in his throat and choke him.

"Partner! This—this—" he mouthed at length.

Whitmer nodded smilingly. "Uh-huh, this is him."

Before Taylor could get his breath again, Ran's lazy drawl broke in:

"Taylor there's somethin' up in the draw what b'longs to you. Better send somebody up for it. Have 'em sing out what they're comin' for, though —jest to save mistakes."

"Somethin' belongin' to me?" sputtered Taylor. "What—how——"

"Uh-huh," drawled Ran. "One of yore pet skunks was climbin' 'round top the cliff theah and fell off and busted his neck. Mebbe you can use his hide for somethin'."

Taylor's face grew even blacker than before. Munson started and for the first time Ran saw him blink.

"Was it—" he began; then his hard mouth clamped shut like a rat trap. Ran's gray-green gaze flickered across his face with interest. There was a haunting resemblance of some sort there.

"I done seen somebody that jigger looks like," he told himself. Aloud he said:

"Guess that's about *all* the bus'ness you got up the draw, Taylor."

There was nothing slow about Cal Taylor; he understood the implication instantly and snarled in his throat:

"Yore usin' that way to tell me you won't sell?"

Ran nodded. "Nope, we won't. Mebbe I'm givin' my partner here a bum steer—that's a purty good-sized hunk of money yore offerin'—but you see he's got sorta clean hands. I don't want him to get 'em dirty."

Taylor's voice was thick with fury, his eyes terrible.

"Hollis, I told yuh before, yore gonna tangle yore rope with mine oncet too often."

"Taylor, we tie hard and fast wheah I come from," Ran replied softly. "When my rope runs out to the end, whatever's in the loop takes a header and takes it hard. Un'stand?"

Taylor gave Ran a long glare, turned abruptly on his heel and plunged through the swinging doors. Munson's face was inscrutable, but Ran read in his single black glance such hate as he would not have thought humanly possible.

"That jigger shore does take a creased thumb serious," mused the cowboy, "but who the hell do I know what looks like him? Somebody I done seen recent, too. Oh, well, what's the difference? I saw lots of rattlesnakes crawlin' 'round out on the prairie of late, come to think on it. Mebbe that's what I'm callin' to mind."

Ran and Whitmer had a couple more drinks. Ran danced a few rounds with an impish girl with merry eyes and a vivid vocabulary.

"Cowboy, you're just six feet of trouble for any girl," she told him, "but it's sure going to be easy to remember you."

The hilarity was at its height when the partners left, but they did not hesitate. They had work to do on the morrow and the problems confronting them required clear heads.

"I been buildin' up a idea," Ran said as they entered the draw. "It——"

"Look there," Whitmer interrupted him. "What's that?"

Ran peered at the reddish glow flickering against the crest of the cliff.

" 'Pears like a fire," he muttered. "What's to burn up there? Or is it reflected from somethin' burnin' lower down?"

Whitmer galvanized into action.

"Come on, feller," he barked, starting to run. "It's the new stamp mill!"

Up the draw they raced, stumbling over rocks, slipping on damp places.

"Where's the watchman?" panted Whitmer. "He oughta be——"

Cr-r-rrack!

A bullet yelled past. Another spun Whitmer's hat from his head. Ran plunged to the ground, knocking Whitmer's legs from under him.

"I'm plugged!" yelled the cowboy. "I'm gunshot! O-o-oh!"

"My God!" screamed Whitmer. "They got you?"

A triumphant curse growled out of the dark ahead. Feet thudded. Two shadowy figures loomed in the starlight.

Ran Hollis' guns streamed fire. Bullet after bullet thudded into the shadowy figures. They went down, kicking and clawing. The cowboy's guns still thundered.

"Thought they'd come to it," he gritted, ejecting spent shells and shoving in fresh cartridges. "C'mon, feller, let's get to that fire."

"You weren't hit?" quavered Whitmer, scrambling to his feet.

"Hell no!" grunted the puncher. "I jest howled thatway to bring them drygulchers to where I could line sights on 'em. Trouble with their kind is they ain't got nothin' to use for brains. There's the fire —top the stamp mill."

Somewhere nearby a man was bawling lustily.

Ran could hear a prodigious thumping. Whitmer swerved aside and raced toward a little building, Ran hard at his heels.

"They locked the watchman in his shanty," panted Whitmer. "We gotta get him out to help."

A heavy iron bar crossed the door of the watchman's shanty. A big padlock was snapped to the staple. Whitmer struggled with it.

"Look out," growled Ran, shoving him aside.

The cowboy hooked slim bronzed fingers under the bar and braced his feet against the door. Great muscles leaped and swelled on back and shoulders and arms. One shirt sleeve split from wrist to shoulder under the surge of mighty tendons.

There was a splintering crash, a screech of complaining iron and Ran sprawled on his back, gripping bar, staple and a section of the door planking. Through the opening burst the cursing watchman, white whiskers bristling.

"The blankety-blank-blankety-blanks slipped up and snapped the lock on me while I was swallerin' a mouthful of chuck!" he bellowed.

"Get the pump goin' and couple on the hose," ordered Whitmer. "That fire'll be too much for us in another minute."

"Them jiggers wasn't so dumb," grunted Ran, unreeling the stout leathern hose. "They set the fire way up high wheah it'd be hard to get at. Listen to her crackle!"

The flames were leaping high before the clanking pump sent a stream of water hissing up toward them. Ran watched it dubiously. Finally he shook his head.

"Won't do," he declared. "We're not gettin' at it right a-tall. Let's see, now."

There was no inner sheathing to the building and the cross pieces to which the outer sheathing was nailed provided a precarious ladder.

"It'll hafta do," Ran nodded. "Shut the water off and gimme that hose."

"You can't climb up there; you'll break yore neck," protested Whitmer.

"Gotta do it. Don't arg'fy. Gimme that hose."

With the nozzle draped over his shoulder the cowboy swarmed up the "ladder." The weight of the sagging hose increased as he climbed and soon it required tremendous effort to draw himself up from one cross piece to the next. Gasping and panting, he reached a narrow beam that ran from wall to wall directly under the sloping roof. He inched along this, dragging the hose after him.

Up there, close to the burning shingles, the heat was terrific. Ran felt his hair crisping, his lungs cooking inside his chest. Perspiration that should have drenched him dried saltily on his skin. His lips were black, his tongue swelling.

"Get that water going," he shouted, his voice

little more than a hoarse croak. Whitmer's answering yell sounded above the crackle of the flames.

The pump clanked. Ran felt the hose swell under his hand. Water gushed from the nozzle. Billowing clouds of steam rolled up to join the smoke as the water struck the flames. Almost instantly, blackened areas appeared. Ran grunted with satisfaction, tipped the nozzle up an instant and was drenched by the water drumming back from the roof over his head.

"That helps like hell!" he muttered, turning the jet on the flames once more. "That steam's damn hard to breathe, though."

The white clouds swirled about him, hiding him from his companions below, blotting out everything from his own sight except the red glare where the flames still persisted stubbornly.

"We're gettin' it!" he exulted. "Lucky the roof beams didn't have time to catch much."

The red glow was dulling swiftly, the steam was thinning out. Ran turned the hose on a final patch of flaming shingles and breathed deep satisfaction as the blaze died. He was abruptly aware of a frenzied shouting from below.

Twisting about he saw what had excited his companions' alarm—the beam which he straddled was burning fiercely.

Ran flipped the hose about, brought the nozzle to bear and the fire vanished with a hiss. But at the same instant he felt the beam shiver and sag beneath him. The burned section cracked ominously. Whitmer yelled a frantic warning.

Dropping the hose, Ran jerked his legs up, got his feet on the beam and scrambled erect. For a split second he stood swaying, fifty feet of absolutely nothing beneath him.

With a sharp crack the beam broke. Down it thundered to the stone floor. Whitmer yelled despairingly.

As the stout timber sagged beneath his feet, Ran leaped, up and out through the black dark, toward another beam ten feet distant. Down he rushed, and for a horrible instant he *"knew"* he had fallen short. Then his reaching arms slammed across the beam.

Madly he clutched the smooth surface, felt one hand jerk free. Two fingers of the other hand hooked over a rough spot and for a moment he hung dangling. Then, groaning with the strain, sweat pouring down his face, he drew himself up and straddled the beam.

"*Mebbe* I'll get to Heaven when I die," he gulped, "like all the good boys is s'posed to, but I was sho' headed the wrong way that time. Hey, down there!"

A joyous answering yell soared up to him. A light winked.

"You all right?" howled Whitmer.

"Restin' easy," Ran told him. "Be with you in a minute."

The fire was completely out and little damage done other than a few holes in the roof and the single broken beam. Nothing that a few hours' work on the part of the mill carpenter could not repair.

"Murder and fire," Ran commented. "Our *amigos* has shore got a fine assortment of tricks in their little bag. Wonder what they'll try next? Well, we got two more skunks for Taylor to skin when he comes after the fust one. Let's see if we can place either one of 'em."

That night Ran wrote a letter to Ray Carrol. The red-haired girl received it many days later. She read it with mixed emotions. She was happy at Ran's chances of making a fortune in the mine, but she was worried about the dangers that hedged him about. She had a long talk with old Wade Harley, with the result that one morning, when the gray mists of the dawn were turning gold and scarlet under the magic hands of the day, she rode away from the Lazy-B ranch. She wore overalls and chaps and a gray woolen shirt. Her bright curls were gathered beneath a broad-brimmed Stetson and her winsome curves were muffled in her nondescript garb. East and north she rode, toward the silver hills and the bright skies of Nevada.

Three weeks later there was a new girl dancing

in one of the biggest saloons of Arivapa, a slim, graceful girl with blue, blue eyes, hair like sunlight on new copper, and a red, red mouth. The miners and the passing cowboys adored her, but there was a reserve about her that held them at arm's length.

"She's jest like what I 'member my mother was when I was a little shaver," said one tough hombre with nine notches on his gun barrel. "Gents, I'm sarvin' notice right now, any hombre what don't treat that li'l lady jest the same as if she *was* my mother is gonna have me lookin' for him, and not with no opry glasses, either!"

Chapter 22

DEATH IN THE DARK

NEITHER Whitmer, the watchman, nor any of the mine workers were able to recognize the two dead incendiaries when they looked them over. They had no better luck with the drygulcher Ran had shot off the cliff top.

"Taylor's too smart to use local men for his ditry work," declared Whitmer. "He'd bring 'em in from the Black Hell country down in Arizona, or from Utah. Yuh can get anybody yuh want killed in this country for ten dollars."

"Yeah?" Ran disagreed. "Well, at bottom prices, our friend Cal has done spent thirty *pesos* and got no results to speak of. At this rate he's liable to run outa killers."

"No danger," grunted Whitmer pessimistically; "there's plenty more. Well, guess I'd better notify Doc McChesney; he's coroner. Nope, there's no danger of him bringin' in a phony verdict. Nobody tells that old hellion what to do—not even Cal Taylor."

The coroner, a rugged frontier doctor of the old school, did not even bother to leave his office.

"Folks ain't got no bus'ness prowlin' 'round on yore property," he told Whitmer. "If they gets theirselves hurt doin' it, it's their lookout. Don't bother me with damphoolishness—I gotta cut Bill Tooley's busted leg off this mawnin' and I ain't had no breakfast and I can't find my saw. Chances are I'll hafta use a choppin' block and a axe. Bill's liable to wish my chloroform waren't all gone."

Work went on in the mine. With pick and drill and blasting powder, the miners drove their tunnels deeper and deeper through the lode. In the new stamp mill the ponderous stamps—tall, upright rods of iron as thick as a man's ankle, and heavily shod with a mass of iron and steel at their lower ends—started their ponderous dance, crushing and pulverizing the ore. After a series of tedious and complicated processes, that crushed ore became portly silver bricks, and a fifth or more of each brick was gold. The Whitmer mine began paying expenses and showing a small profit.

"Things is pickin' up," admitted Ran, "but ev'ry day I'm expectin' our *amigo* Taylor to pull somethin'. I feel it, feller, I feel it!"

The Whitmer mine was a "wet" mine. Ran commented on the fact as he stood in one of the drifts watching the dark stream that gurgled past in a side ditch.

"Plenty water down here, partner."

"Uh-huh, there is," nodded Whitmer; "it keeps the pumps busy pullin' it outa the sump, but it ain't no good for anything. Too much acid and mineral salts. Foams in boilers and won't make steam, and you can't drink it. Just a damn nuisance. The Mescalero's got even more than we have. I hear that new diggin', the one so close to ours, is wetter'n hell."

"Come to think on it, I ain't heard their picks and drills through the wall for a day or two," Ran remarked. "Mebbe they've given that drift up as a bad job."

"Mebbe," admitted Whitmer without interest. "Well, let's be gettin' top-side; we'll look the new drift over tomorrow."

The new drift was the deepest yet attempted. It was also nearest Taylor's Mescalero mine. Ran and Whitmer found a half-dozen miners there busily driving ahead with power drills and giant powder.

"Jest gettin' ready to set off a blast at the head of the tunnel," the foreman told them. "Wanta wait and see what she brings down?"

Ran nodded. "Guess we might as well."

The miners came trooping back from the head of the drift. One lingered, fiddling with his cap lamp.

"Fire!" he bawled suddenly. "Fi-i-ire!" and came trotting along the tunnel.

"She's lit," said the foreman. "Let's get in the clear, gents."

In the black dark at the head of the drift, lighted fuses writhed and sputtered like fiery snakes. Swiftly they burned their lengths, the showering sparks vanishing into the drill holes with sullen little puffs. There was a moment of tingling silence, then a frightful blaze of red and yellow flame, a vast mushroom burst of smoke and a thunder-roll of sound. The black wall at the head of the drift seemed to dissolve. Down it crashed, thudding and splintering.

Ran and Whitmer, snugged in a niche some distance along the tunnel, heard the boom of the blast and the rumble of the falling rock. Those sounds were expected and explainable. But utterly unexpected and, for the moment, unexplainable was the growling roar that followed. They could not see the writhing, frothing monster that leaped through the opening the dynamite had made in the apparently solid drift head.

The foreman, a little nearer the blast, gave a startled yell.

"Water!" he howled. "Back—outa this—we've busted open the ocean!"

In headlong flight, the miners raced through the

drift. After them pounded Ran, Whitmer and the foreman. Before they had gone a score of paces the flood was upon them. Ran felt himself caught up as in giant arms and hurled forward. He took a deep breath the instant before the icy black water rolled over him.

For several moments he could do nothing to combat the hurtling current. The rolling crest of the wave whirled and buffeted him. Part of the time he was on the surface, part beneath. He struck out strongly, trying to govern his movements; but not until the boiling crest had passed over and by him did he meet with any success. The following water, although it ran like a mill race, was less turbulent and he was quickly something other than a chip tossed aimlessly about.

"Gotta get over to the side and swarm up the shorin' timbers," he sputtered; "be lucky if I don't bust my brains out 'gainst one."

He started a slant across the narrow tunnel, groping for one of the great upright beams. Something barged him and he instinctively clutched it. His fingers closed on sodden clothing. The wearer was limp and unconscious.

"Somebody what can't swim," panted the cowboy. "Now ain't this one helluva note? How'm I gonna climb up a straight log with this jigger on my hands?"

It never occurred to him to let the unconscious "jigger" go.

During his tussle with the drowning man, the current had again swept him to the middle of the tunnel. Once again he started the slant that would bring him to the shoring timbers, supporting the limp head with one hand and paddling strongly with the other.

Suddenly he reached the timbers, and had all the breath knocked out of him. He careened off the first upright but managed to get a grip on the next one with his free hand.

"Now for it," he gulped. "This is gonna be hell!"

It was. To climb the smooth, wet upright to the first cross piece with nothing to bother him would have been no mean feat. To do so with a raging torrent tearing at him and a half-drowned man encumbering him appeared to be on the wrong side of the impossible; but Ran knew he could not endure the bite of that icy water much longer.

"No tellin' how much of it there is," he muttered. "Well, heah goes."

He gripped the timber with his knees, wedging the unconscious form against it, head above water. Then he managed to get the big handkerchief from about his neck. With the handkerchief he bound the man's hands together. He looped the bound arms around his neck. Then, with the unconscious man hanging onto his back, he began to climb the upright.

Inch by painful inch, gripping the timber with bleeding hands and raw knees. At first the current almost tore him from his hold but after an eternity of exhausting effort he got above its grip. Shaking and panting, his heart hammering his chest with blacksmith blows, his lungs nigh to bursting, he reached the cross piece. With a last vestige of strength that was really nothing but the iron of a will that held on when there was nothing else left to hold on with, he pulled himself and his burden onto the cross piece. For several minutes he sprawled on the beam, gasping, retching, crushed by the weight of the still form on his back, but lacking the strength to remove it. Finally he was able to edge the unconscious man over, get the bound arms from around his neck and drape him across the beam.

"That'll let some of the water run outa him," muttered the exhausted cowboy. "Hope he ain't dead, after all the trouble I went to with him. That'd be one helluva note!"

Five minutes later a gasping groan and a weak flopping reassured Ran.

"Comin' outa it, eh?" he said. "Heah, lemme thump yore back a bit."

Followed another groan, then the voice of Tom Whitmer——

"Ran, what the hell happened?"

"Leapin' lizards, it's you!" marvelled the puncher. "What happened? Oh, nothin' much. Water washed us up onto this log, I guess; anyhow we're heah. If that damn water ever stops runnin' we'll trail our ropes to the cage and go top-side."

The water stopped running after a while and the partners sloshed through it, waist-deep, to the shaft and were drawn up in the soaking cage.

"Helluva job of pumpin' to do," the drift foreman told them, "and six men got drowned, near as I can figger. It's hell!"

The Whitmer mine abruptly stopped paying expenses or making a profit.

"Well, she's cleaned out again," said Whitmer, many days later, "and I'm just about cleaned out, too. Hardly enough left to buy grub and pay wages the rest of this month."

Ran inspected the head of the drift, from where the unexpected flood had come. He was pulled to the surface drenched, dirty, and mad as a wet hen.

"Taylor took a trick this time, all right," he told Whitmer. "Smart as hell, that blankety-blank."

"Taylor?" exclaimed Whitmer. "What'd Taylor have to do with it?"

"We busted inter that new tunnel the Mescalero's been drivin' the past month," said Ran.

"Yes, I figured we did that," replied Whitmer, "but I don't see——"

"Go down there and you'll see damn quick," interrupted Ran. "Of all the blankety-blank-blanked ornery tricks! That sidewinder would hawgtie his grandma and plant her in a ant hill!

"It's like this, Tom," he went on in a calmer voice, "the horned toad run that tunnel to wheah he knowed our drift would bust inter it sooner or later. It's a big wide tunnel. You know how wet the Mescalero is?"

"Uh-huh," nodded Whitmer, "plenty wet."

"And that new tunnel's the wettest part of all," went on Ran; "water jest pourin' inter it in a dozen places. Well Taylor walled up the front end of that tunnel—it's set quite a bit higher than our drift—and let her fill plumb fulla water. When we busted in, as he callated we would, we got the water.

"And the wuss part of it," he added, "is that we can't prove a darn thing. Taylor has a perfect right to run a tunnel so long as he follers his own lode, and if he makes a little mistake and runs it a mite too clost to ourn—well, he jest made a mistake, that's all. And he's got a right to wall a tunnel up and keep water outa his other drifts, too. Nope, we can't do a thing. He took a trick this time, that's all."

Whitmer nodded moodily. "Uh-huh. Taylor can afford to run tunnels and pump water. We can't. Murder, fire and water! What next?"

But it was not Cal Taylor but inscrutable fate that struck the next blow at the Whitmer mine.

Chapter 23

THE BLIND LEAD

RAN and Whitmer were in the little office at the stamp mill when the drift foreman clumped in, his face lined with worry.

"I wish you gents would come below a bit and take a look at things," he said.

Something in the man's voice brought the partners to their feet.

"More trouble?" demanded Whitmer nervously.

"Can't tell," said the foreman, "but it don't look so good. Come on down and see for yoreself."

All three men were silent as the cage shot down the black shaft. Still wordless, the foreman clumped along the main tunnel that plowed through the lode. Rock was coming down at the head of the drift, but there was a tense air noticeable among the men working there. The foreman stopped and began picking up fragments of the rock.

"Take a look at it," he said, thrusting out a handful of lumps.

Whitmer took the fragments, glanced at them,

wet one with his tongue and peered closer. Silently he passed the chip to Ran. The cowboy stared at it with knitted brows.

"It shore ain't the same as we been gettin'," he decided.

Whitmer nodded and picked up more fragments.

"How long has this been goin' on?" he asked the foreman.

"Since yesterday. I thought at fust it might be jest a fault and didn't mention it, but the rock kept changin' more and more and I thought I'd better call you."

"Right," said Whitmer. "Now listen: start a stream of this rock goin' to the assayer. Get reports on its mineral content—keep gettin' reports as you drive ahead—and start drivin' tunnels to the right and left. Mebbe this *is* jest a fault or a slip and you'll pick up the lode again."

"Okay," said the foreman, but Ran caught a pessimistic note in his voice.

"That jigger figgers right now the vein's jest plain peterin' out," muttered the cowboy. "Well, all we can do is go ahead and see what's next."

Three days later Whitmer sat in the mill office, staring at a sheaf of assayer's reports. The assays showed a steadily dwindling mineral content in the Whitmer mine rock.

"Here's the latest one," he said, passing the

greasy sheet to Ran, "and it shows about as much gold or silver as you'd find in a chunk busted outa a grindstone. Feller, the lode's done petered out."

"Mebbe them tunnels to left and right'll pick it up again," suggested Ran hopefully.

Whitmer shook his head. "Nope, there isn't a sign—absolutely nothing to show a fault or a slip. The lode was just a sorta pocket affair, short and shallow. There ain't enough metal to make what we got wuth workin'. Besides, I'm flat busted and you can't work a silver mine 'thout capital."

"And you can't borrow on one that don't show fust-class assay reports," added Ran. "Well, partner, now what?"

Whitmer's face was haggard from work, worry and lack of sleep, but he managed a grin.

"Pick and shovel for me and a hoss and a rope for you, I guess. Feller, we ain't gonna be millionaires yet a while. Looks like Cal Taylor got the best of that trade, after all."

It never occurred to either of the young men to go back on the trade, now that the mine was proved worthless, although they could easily have done so, controlling the water source as they did. With them a bargain was a bargain, even a losing one with a treacherous and unfair enemy.

Ran unbuckled his money belt and drew it from

under his shirt. He shook the contents onto the table and divided the money into two equal sums.

"Here you are, feller," he said, shoving one pile of gold pieces toward Whitmer.

"Share and share alike," he said in a tone of finality as the other started to protest. "When we agreed to be partners, that meant partners the whole way. We got enough *pesos* here to keep us goin' a few days. Mebbe somethin' will turn up. Now let's amble to town and get ourselves a drink; we need it!"

They found Arivapa boiling with excitement. It was payday at the big mines, but not even that agreeable fact could account for the hullabaloo that had broken loose. They speedily learned what was in the air.

"It's the Mescalero," an excited bartender told them. "They've made a strike there, the richest ever! Mescalero rock's always been good payin' rock, but never like it is now. Why it beats anythin' Virginia or Gold Hill had at their best. Comstock Lode, hell! Why the Comstock is jest chicken feed compared to this! Look, I'll show you."

From a shelf under the bar he produced a lump of black, decomposed rock which could be crumbled in the hand almost like a baked potato. He improvised a makeshift mortar from a cracked dish and used a bottle as a pestle. He ground up the ore with his crude implements and washed it out in a horn spoon. Ran and Whitmer glared speechless at the marvelous result.

There was exhibited a thick sprinkling of gold and particles of native silver!

"Didja ever see anythin' like that?" demanded the barkeep. "If Cal Taylor fell down a mud hole he'd come out covered with diamonds! Have a drink on the house, gents. Jest lookin' at that stuff makes me feel expansive."

Ran and Whitmer drank soberly, still regarding the results of the bartender's "assay." Whitmer spoke first, a trifle bitterly.

"Looks like bein' crooked as hell is a payin' prop'sition."

Ran shook his head. "Nope," he replied decidedly, "it ain't. It jest looks that way, at times. Square dealin' pays in the end."

"Mebbe yore right," grunted Whitmer, "but I'm beginnin' to sorta have doubts."

Ran turned to the bartender.

"You got a little piece of that rock to spare?" he asked. "I'd sorta like to have it for a souvenir."

"Shore," said the barkeep, "here's one you can have. I packed away a whole pocketful. Heah tell Taylor's stopped folks carryin' off specimens, though; rock's wuth money. Why a sixteen-hundred-pound parcel sold jest as it lay at the shaft mouth for *a dollar a pound*. Feller what bought it is figgerin' on packin' it on mules over the mountains to San Francisco. Says he'll make plenty profit. Gents, she shore is rich."

That night in the cabin, while Whitmer pretended to read a month-old San Francisco newspaper, Ran puzzled over the bit of black "rock." He examined it with a glass, inspected it in different lights and from different points of view. Over and over he muttered to himself:

"It's *not* Mescalero rock!"

"Oh, what the hell's the difference!" growled Whitmer finally. "We don't own it, whatever it is. *I'm* goin' to bed."

Long after his partner's heavy breathing denoted that he slept, Ran Hollis sat at the table, brooding over the lump of ore. Bits of mining lore passed through his head, and half remembered stories of queer happenings and unusual lodes. Finally he stood up, decision written on his face, and delivered to himself an ultimatum:

"I'm gonna get a look down that Mescalero shaft if I get shot doin' it."

Quietly, so as not to disturb Whitmer, he blew out the light and left the cabin. There were plenty of chances to get shot in the course of what he proposed doing—that he well knew—but he was firmly resolved to take the risk.

"Today bein' payday, there won't be no night shift workin'," he reasoned. "Oughtn't to be anybody 'round but a watchman or two, and I can duck them."

With the greatest caution he approached the Mescalero mine. His object was the building which housed the shaft. Peering through a dusty window he saw the watchman puttering about. Otherwise the building, and those near it, were silent and deserted.

"That feller'll be amblin' around to look the other places over 'fore long," he decided, and settled himself to wait with such patience as he could muster.

Finally the watchman left the shaft building and disappeared in the direction of the main engine house. Ran slipped into the deserted building and glided to the shaft. He paused at the edge of the yawning pit and glanced at the slim shadow of the rope that wound about the huge drum under the roof and vanished into the blackness of the shaft. The cage was resting at the bottom of the shaft, a hundred feet below.

"And if I try to pull it up, the noise of the engine runnin'll bring that watchman jigger back like a shot, and hell only knows who else," muttered the puncher. "Well, this is a chance I hadn't figgered on, but I gotta take it."

He crouched on the lip of the shaft, muscles tense. Then like a coiled spring he straightened and leaped, straight out across the ghastly chasm.

Slam! He struck the rope and bounded back, legs twining, hands clutching. He got a slippery grip on the rope and shot down into the black dark. With hands and knees he checked his progress, losing much skin in the process. Still going fast, he struck the cage roof with a crash, lost his hold and rolled off to the bottom of the shaft. For a moment he lay gasping, then he scrambled to his feet, took a cap lamp from his pocket, lighted it and hooked it into place. The black mouth of the deserted main tunnel swallowed him up.

Just as dawn was streaking the eastern sky with glory he returned to the shaft. The cage was operated by levers at the bottom of the shaft as well as the top and Ran started it rising. The wrathful watchman met him as he stepped from the cage.

"Who are you and what you doin' down in that mine?" demanded the watchman.

Ran pointed to a corner of the room. "There's yore boss, Mr. Taylor; you better ask him."

As the watchman whirled to look, Ran ducked past him and skipped out the door. Curses fol-

lowed him down the hill, but nothing more dangerous. Hot, dirty, and blazing with excitement he
banged open the door of the cabin in the draw.

"Tom," he yelled at the startled Whitmer, "we're
rich! We're wuth millions! Tom, *it's a blind lead!*"

Chapter 24

TAYLOR STRIKES

For an astounded moment Whitmer stared owl-ishly. Finally he mouthed words:

"Say it again!"

Ran laughed happily, his green eyes glowing like fern-shadowed water in the sunlight.

"It's a blind lead," he repeated, "a perfect blind lead—hangin' wall—foot wall—clay casin's—everythin' complete!"

Whitmer whistled softly and leaped out of bed.

"You really mean it—you really mean the Mescalero's new strike is a blind lead, the kind of a ledge that never shows on the surface and is only discovered by accident, like in the course of driving a tunnel or sinking a shaft?"

"That's it," declared Ran. "It's not Mescalero rock a-tall. It's another vein, holdin' its independent through the Mescalero lode and cuttin' it diagonally. It so darn near parallels the Mescalero vein for a bit that it's no wonder they were fooled inter thinkin' it was jest their lode gettin' rich; but there it is, enclosed in its own puffectly marked out casin'-rocks and clay."

Whitmer whooped exultantly.

"Then she's public property and anybody can take possession of it, record it and establish ownership and forbid the Mescalero people to take out any more of the rock. They can work their own lode, but they'll hafta leave the blind lead alone."

"That's how she stands," nodded Ran. "That's minin' law. We'll locate the blind lead for ourselves, right away, and let Taylor snort."

"Oh, he'll snort, all right!" chuckled Whitmer. *"Will* he snort! C'mon, feller, let's get goin'. Yore the only man in camp what had the brains to figger this thing out straight. C'mon, let's cash in on it."

Before noon the notice of location was up and duly spread on the recorder's books. Ran Hollis and Tom Whitmer were, beyond all argument, the new owners of the Mescalero blind lead.

Not that Cal Taylor didn't feel like arguing.

"He's wild," Whitmer told Ran. "Barkeep told me he said he'd shoot us if we tried to go inter the mine to do the location work the laws of the district require."

Ran's face tightened grimly, but Whitmer flung out a staying hand.

"No use to go on the prod," he laughed, "it's done been taken care of. The word got around and this aft'noon a Vigilance Committee called on friend Taylor. They told him that every miner in the district was back of the Committee and that if he violated minin' law and interfered with us doin' our location work they'd hang him. Taylor backed down in a hurry."

Ran shook his head. "Funny, the way these minin' camps looks at things. A jigger can commit murder, steal, and pull up green corn, and nothin's done about it; but let him bust a minin' law and he stretches rope. Well, it works in our favor this time, all right."

He rolled a cigarette and puffed thoughtfully.

"We got ten days to do the location work, haven't we?" he asked Whitmer.

"Yes," Whitmer replied. "If we don't do it within ten days, the property is forfeited and anybody can seize it and relocate it. But there's nothin' to worry about. Just so one of us does a day's work with pick and shovel before the ten days are up. We'll take care of that, all right."

Ran still puffed thoughtfully at his cigarette.

"Tom," he said at length, "this is a big thing and hard to swing. What we need is a third pardner— a man we can trust, one with money and influence. We're gonna need backin' 'fore we're done with this, feller."

Whitmer nodded agreement:

"I can see where yore right, but who the hell can
we get? Do you know anybody with all them quali-
fications?"

"Nope," replied Ran, "I don't; but you do."

"Me?" exclaimed Whitmer.

"Uh-huh, you."

"Who, you aggravatin' jughead?"

"Nobody but yore Uncle Pete."

Whitmer grunted his scorn:

"Uncle Pete! Peter Whitmer! Hell, didn't I
tell you he didn't have no use for me?"

"Uh-huh," countered Ran, "and you once told me
he'd let *me* bust aigs in his Sunday hat."

Whitmer leaped to his feet, eyes glowing.

"By gosh, feller, you've hit it!" he exclaimed.
"Uncle Pete'd take to you like a hog to a second
helpin'. He'd even put up with me if he found me
'sociatin' with a salty *hombre* like you. I'll give you
a letter to him and you can do the rest. He'll talk
to you, all right."

Ran did some quick figuring.

"I can make the trip to Salt Lake City and back
in a coupla weeks," he decided. "I'll foller the
Pony Express route. I can ride up to that station
to the nawth of heah and get a line on it. It's the
shortest route, all right. You can do the location
work and get things in shape heah as best you can.
I'll line up Uncle Pete and get him back of us.

Then we won't hafta worry 'bout Taylor or any other crooked hellion."

Not until he was actually riding toward ᴡ.. lt Lake City did Ran realize how much he had missed the jingle of harness, the creak of saddle leather and the feel of a good horse between his knees. He grinned happily, feasting his eyes on the rich beauty of the flower jeweled prairie and breathing deep of the clean, sun drenched air.

"Mebbe I'm on the way to bein' a minin' millionaire," he chuckled, "but one thing's certain—jest as soon as I get 'nough money ahaid I'm gonna invest in a fust-class cow outfit. I got too darn much grass rope and saddle leather and hoss-flesh mixed up in my blood to stay from the range over long."

He found Salt Lake City a neat, thrifty town lying in the edge of a vast level plain and under the curving wall of mighty mountains whose heads were hidden in the clouds. He had been six days making the journey from Arivapa.

Peter Whitmer's name was well known and Ran experienced no difficulty locating him. The old Mormon elder had a formidable reputation in the town and Ran approached the door of his office with some misgiving. He knocked, wondering what kind of reception he would get.

"Come in, blankety-blank-blank it!" roared a thundering bass that shook the building from shingles to foundation. Ran entered and stared at a great sultry disk fringed about with flaming red whiskers. Peter Whitmer's face was weather beaten to the color of mahogany, studded with warts and seamed with scars. His snapping black eyes glared out from under shaggy brows. His nose was a gnarled crag, his chin vast and square, his mouth wide and good humored. He was stalwart and portly, with a crinkly mane of snow-white hair sweeping back from his big dome-shaped forehead.

"What the blankety-blank-blank do *you* want?" he inquired kindly.

Ran grinned and his green eyes were sunny. He liked Peter Whitmer, immediately and without reservation.

"I got a letter from your nephew, Tom Whitmer," he stated.

Old Peter exploded a regular geyser stream of profanity. "That good-for-nothin' young so-and-so!" he concluded, "what does *he* want? His dad's all right, but he's no good."

"Mr. Whitmer, I'm sorry to bring bad news, but yore brother's daid," Ran stated quietly.

"Dead! Joe dead?"

Ran saw the old man's lips tremble and his knuckles whiten as he gripped the top of the table behind which he sat.

"How'd he come to die?"

Ran pulled up a chair and sat down, facing Peter Whitmer.

"I'll jest tell you the whole story," he said, "and 'fore you get on the prod too much 'gainst Tom Whitmer, let me tell you what all he's done and what all he's up against."

Ten minutes later the tale of Arivapa and the Whitmer mine was finished and Peter Whitmer was pounding the table top with a fist like a ham.

"Shore I'll throw in with you!" he roared. "I'll show that blankety-blank Taylor a thing or two, 'fore I'm through with him. I got a notion to ask Brigham to send out a flock of Destroyin' Angels to deal with him, even if he is in Nevada 'stead of Utah. When they get through with him theah wouldn't even be a meal left for a buzzard."

Ran, remembering some of the stories he had heard concerning the Destroying Angels, the official executioners and avengers of the early Mormon Church, was inclined to agree with him.

"A fine boy, that nevvy of mine," added old Peter. "A chip off the old block. Blood'll tell, young man, blood'll tell!"

Ran smothered a grin behind his hand.

"It shore will," he agreed. "He looks like you, too, Mr. Whitmer."

Old Peter beamed.

"Now about money you'll need," he began. "I'll —what the blankety-blank is that racket out theah?"

A clatter of high heels sounded in the outer office, the door was flung violently open and a girl leaped into the room—a girl with blue, blue eyes and red curls flying in wild abandon. She was haggard with fatigue, but her voice rang like silver bells.

"*Ray!*" yelled Ran Hollis. "How—what— where——"

Ray Carrol silenced him with an imperative gesture of one little sun-golden hand.

"I've been trying to catch you all the way," she cried. "Unless you get back to Arivapa in time to do the location work on the blind lead you'll lose it. The work won't be done unless you do it and the mine will be relocated. Taylor's got his outfit all primed to jump it as soon as the ten days are up."

Ran leaped to his feet.

"Tom! what happened to Tom?" he demanded.

"It happened the morning after you left," Ray explained. "Tom was going to do the location work that day. He stepped out of the cabin just as it was getting light and stepped into a bear trap somebody had planted in front of the cabin with leaves and dirt over it. When Watson, the foreman, found him, his leg was badly lacerated. The bone wasn't broken but he can't set foot on the ground. Doctor McChesney says he won't be able to for weeks."

Peter Whitmer swore until the air about his head was a dark purple.

"More of that blankety-blank Taylor's work!" he concluded.

"Yes," Ray agreed, "but there isn't any proving it. That snake-eyed Bat Munson was headed in the direction of the draw the night before with a bundle under his arm; but nobody could say for sure the bundle was a bear trap."

Ran was thinking swiftly. "Four days," he muttered, "four days left. I took six to get here, but I didn't hustle. There's a chance, a darn slim one, but a chance."

He turned to old Peter.

"You got good hosses?" he demanded. "Or can you get hold of good ones? Mine is 'bout tuckered by his trip, I'll need two, one to ride and the other to lead. When the fust one gives out, I'll use the second."

"I'll be right behind you, Ran!" cried Ray.

Chapter 25

THE "PONY EXPRESS"

DAWN! With the sun pushing its flaming disc up over the edge of the world and flooding the level prairie with golden light. Larks sang, roses shook the dew from their petals, a whisper of song that was the morning wind played the grass blades like a many-stringed violin. The sky deepened from tenderest pink to perfect blue.

Out of the arms of the sunlight thundered a lone horseman. Foam flecked the shiny black coat of the splendid horse he bestrode. The cayuse's nostrils flared, his eyes were gorged with blood. He seemed to drive himself forward through sheer power of will.

His rider was in little better shape. Haggard, bleary-eyed, gray-faced with fatigue, Ran Hollis crouched in the saddle, the lean muscles rippling along his clamped jaw. His lips were drawn back from his teeth. He breathed jerkily.

"We ain't gonna make it, hoss," he mumbled. "You'll be done fer in another ten miles, and I can't

241

walk the rest of the way in time. They're gonna beat us by twenty miles, hoss!"

On thundered the black horse, the second of the two magnificent animals provided by Peter Whitmer. Ran crouched lower, peering ahead.

Suddenly he straightened. A huddle of buildings had leaped into view as they rounded a hillock. He slumped again as he recognized them.

"Jest the Pony Express station," he grunted. "Don't mean nothin' to us. No chance to get a hoss there—only a pony-rider's allowed to use them."

As he swept toward the station he noted activity about the buildings. Men, mere dots in the distance, were running to and fro. He saw two dots scurrying forth with a larger dot between them. He stared at them wonderingly. Suddenly he swore a startled oath. He twisted in the saddle and glanced back the way he had come. Again his gaze fixed on the three dots, now rapidly growing larger as his flying bronk cut down the distance.

"They think I'm the pony-rider," he mumbled. "They've got the pony-rider's hoss all saddled and bridled and waitin'. Gosh if I could only borrer——"

The muttered words died on his lips as sudden white-hot inspiration flashed through his brain.

"It's wuth tryin'," he exulted. "It's wuth takin' a chance!"

Crouching still lower, he swept the wide hat from

his head and let it fall to the ground. Pony-riders never wore anything on their heads heavier than a close-fitting skull-cap.

"Take it fast a mite longer, hoss," he begged. "You'll be all set for oats in another ten minutes, if things work out."

At the Pony Express station, the hostlers holding the champing thoroughbred tensed with expectation.

"Here he comes!" one of them exclaimed, "right on top of us. All right, Bill."

Into the station thundered a magnificent black horse, dimly seen in a cloud of dust. His rider pulled him up with sliding hoofs and clashing bit.

"All away!" shouted the hostlers as the rider leaped to the ground and swung aboard the waiting horse. Away he thundered, in another cloud of dust. Behind him sounded a startled yell:

"Bill! that ain't Crawford! That ain't the pony-rider! What the bloomin' blue blazin'——"

Ran did not hear any more. The wafer of a saddle, totally unlike anything he had ever used, was giving him trouble; but he soon mastered it, and the feel of the fresh horse between his thighs renewed his strength.

"Now if I can jest have luck at the next station," he exulted. "Oughta be jest as easy as the last one, too. I must be ridin' darn close to the reg'lar pony-rider's schedule. Chances are good they'll get the hoss ready at the next station soon as they see me comin'.

" 'Spose I'll get me inter a jam for this trick," he muttered a little later, "but the superintendent was so darn pleased when he learned I'd downed that sidewinder what drygulched Rappold that I got a notion he'll pull me outa it when he finds out how things stand."

The horse, a tall roan, was literally flying. Trained to service in the Pony Express, it was accustomed to giving its utmost for the ten-mile stretch. It would be practically exhausted when it reached the next station, but it would be there in an astonishingly short time.

Ran peered ahead anxiously as the station hove into view. Then he swore happily. The hostlers perceiving the lone rider sweeping down upon them, were leading out the pony-rider's fresh horse. These men were more observant than the last, however. As Ran swung to the ground one of them yelled a warning.

"Who the hell are you?" he shouted, leaping in front of the puncher.

Ran let him have one that started from the knee. Down he went. The other hostler drew a gun and shot, but Ran went under the bullet and hooked an iron-hard fist to his jaw before he could fire again. Before either hostler had recovered, the cowboy was racing away from the station, turning his horse's

head away from the Pony Express route and toward
Arivapa, six miles to the south.

"Gonna make it! Gonna make it!" he exulted
as he sighted the smoke cloud above the town. A
little later the huddle of buildings on the mountain
flank appeared.

Up the main street of the town roared the "Pony
Express." Before Doc McChesney's office, a scant
hundred yards from the Mescalero mine, Ran pulled
the plunging bronk to a halt. Old Doc came running out in answer to his shouts.

"How's Tom?" Ran demanded.

"He's all right!" bellowed Doc. "Leg's healin'
fine. Get inter that mine, you blankety-blank work
dodger, and do yore location chore. This is yore
last day and you gotta put in ten hours. So that
fine little gal got to yuh in time, did she?"

Suddenly realizing how utterly tired he was, Ran
stumbled to the mine shaft. Behind him trotted old
Doc McChesney, a buffalo gun cradled in the crook
of his arm.

"I'm jest gonna hang around and see that nobody
interferes with yore doin' that work," declared Doc.
"You ain't in the best of shape. I got a bottle of
likker on my hip, too."

The hill-top on which the shaft-house rested was
black with men. As Ran hove into view, some
cursed. Others cheered.

"There won't be no relocatin' heah t'day, you

hombres," grunted Doc. "You might as well go home."

Most of the crowd decided to do so, good-naturedly enough. One heavily armed group scowled blackly but evidently did not care to argue with Ran's Colts and Doc's buffalo gun, backed as they were by overwhelming public opinion.

That day in the Mescalero mine ever after remained a vague nightmare to Ran Hollis. He dimly recalled swinging pick or shovel through an eternity of aching hours, with every nerve and muscle crying out its intolerable weariness. His eyes, heavy from sleepless nights, closed time and again, even while his tools thudded mechanically against the crumbling quartz. At last, from afar off, he heard Doc McChesney shout——

"That's enough. You done put in plenty of time and done plenty of work to hold her. Knock off, son, knock off."

As Ran straightened his weary back he drawled:

"Doc, you walked inter here a sorta poverty-stricken range sawbones. Yore walkin' out part owner in a helluva rich mine, and if you start argu-fyin' with me 'bout it, I'll tie yore whiskers in a knot and make you swaller 'em. Let's go top-side."

The hill-top was deserted save for a few idlers when they reached the surface. Taylor's relocaters were nowhere in sight.

Seated outside the shaft-house door was a tired,

lonely little figure, a gun in her lap. "I got here about an hour ago," Ray told Ran.

"If it hadn't been for you, honey, them side-winders woulda won out," Ran declared.

They had a cup of coffee and a sandwich in Doc's office. Then they headed for the cabin in the draw. Twilight was falling when they reached it. Hand on the latch, they suddenly paused. Voices were sounding inside the cabin. Ran recognized Whitmer's, and another.

"I'm damned if I can figger out why yore doin' this, Taylor," Whitmer was saying, "but I'll hafta admit it's white of you, if yore on the level."

Then Cal Taylor's voice, smooth and oily——

"I jest been feelin' bad 'bout things, Whitmer. I didn't do what you think I did, but I did try to run you out. You can't blame me for relocatin' the blind lead when you and yore partner didn't do the work. If I hadn't done it, somebody else would. And ain't I showin' I'm on the level by offerin' to make the company a three-way partnership with you and Hollis and myself owners? What more can I do? Now you jest sign these papers and I'll hustle down and file them 'fore the office closes."

"I shore ain't got nothin' to lose by doin' it," admitted Whitmer. "All right, here goes."

A pen scratched on paper as Ran hurled the door open and went across the room in a single bound.

Whitmer sat propped up in bed, pen in hand. On his lap rested a closely written sheet.

Ran ripped the paper from beneath the pen and tore it to shreds. Then he turned his white-hot rage on Cal Taylor, by whose side sat Bat Munson.

"You sneakin', drygulchin', double-dealin' skunks!" roared the cowboy. "If this ain't the best ever! You knowed I was doin' the location work on the lead and you sneak down heah and try to hornswoggle Tom inter signin' up a partnership agreement that would let you in on the ground floor! Taylor, I've a notion to slit yore neck and ram yore leg through it!"

Mouthing curses, Taylor scrambled to his feet. Ran hit him, right and left, with everything he had, and he went down like a poled ox.

"Look out for Munson!" screamed Ray.

Ran saw steel flicker in the bony man's hand. He ducked under the plunging knife and closed with Munson. The knife tinkled to the floor as he twisted the other's wrist, and then Munson's long fingers were clamped on his throat and he was fighting for his life.

"That was my brother you shot there on the clifftop!" screamed Munson, foam flecking his writhing lips. "I'm gonna tear yore damn heart out, an' eat it!"

Munson's hand was like a band of spring steel. Ran tore at his wrist and struck with his other hand.

Back and forth they reeled panting and gasping.
Red lights were flaming before the cowboy's eyes.
His lungs were bursting. A frantic lunge and the
fighters reeled through the open door. Close by
the creek whisked past and plunged into the bottom-
less gulf.

Ran felt his last strength going. He had reached
the cabin almost exhausted, and Munson was no
weakling. Those long fingers kept clamping tighter
and tighter.

With a final desperate effort, Ran hurled himself
backward to the ground. Munson's fingers tore free
from his throat and the cowboy grasped both his
wrists and kicked upward with all his might, legs
rigid as bars of iron.

Over the puncher's head flew Munson, screaming
in his agony. His cry of pain turned to a yell of
awful terror as he cleared the lip of the chasm and
shot downward. The yell thinned to a whimpering
wail that threaded away to a dead whisper of
sound. Ran glanced at the hissing waterfall and
shuddered.

"You shore oughta make a big splash when you
hit Hell," he apostrophised the vanished Munson.

Ran found Taylor sitting up and looking pretty
sick. The cowboy motioned to the open door.

"Get out," he told Taylor, "and keep goin'. I'd
oughter shoot you and save us the trouble you'll

cause us again some day, but I guess I jest ain't built that way. *Vamos!*"

Without a word, Taylor slunk out into the night.

And far, far beneath the starlit world, through gloomy caverns that would never know the sun, a white-faced limp thing hurtled swiftly toward the distant ocean. Bat Munson, murderer, drygulcher, paid killer, was making a long, long one-way trip.

Grinning happily at each other, the two partners solemnly shook hands.

"Feller, how's it feel to be a millionaire?" chuckled Whitmer.

Ran Hollis' eyes were looking beyond the dingy walls of the cabin—looking at mile upon mile of flower-dotted prairie with the blue shadow of the wind rippling the grasses. He flung a long arm around Ray's supple waist and drew her close.

"What I'm thinkin' 'bout," he said, "is jest what color of ranchhouse would go best with red hair!"

THE END

www.ingramcontent.com/pod-product-compliance
Lightning Source LLC
Chambersburg PA
CBHW010805250626
47156CB00010B/3005